No Good Turn Goes Unpunished

Robyn C Rye

Published by robyncrye, 2023.

Also by Robyn C Rye

Farnsworth Sisters
Marrying a Rogue
Rescuing Hannah

The Buckingham Sisters
Lady Maggie's Challenge
Layla's Unwanted Husband

The Evans Family
Sometimes Love is not Enough
Still the One
Moving Forward

Standalone
One More Chance
Lady Jayne's Reputation
Third Time's the Charm
Can't Stop Loving You

The Marriage Scam
An Unlikely Match
Searching For You
The Unexpected Suitor
The Lady and the Duke
Starting Over
An Unforgettable Stranger
The Duke's Revenge
The Temporary Wife
Against The Odds
Betrayed
No Good Turn Goes Unpunished
Lady Eloise's Soldier
Lillian's Forbidden Beau
Remember Me
Always Second Best
When One Door Closes
Coming Home to You
Chasing Shadows
Fool Me Once
Deserting Lady Audrey
My Unlikely Saviour
Lies and Deception
A New Beginning
Julia's Second Chance
The Hidden Enemy
The Maiden's Redemption
Miss Elizabeth's Season

Table of Contents

Copyright © 2024 by Robyn C Rye

Author's Message

As a reader, you may wonder why some words seem misspelt, but as an Australian writer, I use English spellings rather than American ones. So, NO! I am not a poor speller, and I have used the spell check, but with an Australian slant.

I loved recounting the story of Kennedy and Ben, and I hope you enjoyed the unfolding tale of their trials and successes.

If you enjoyed the book and have a moment, I would appreciate a brief review on the page or site where you purchased it. Your help in spreading the word is appreciated. Reviews from readers like you make a massive difference in helping new readers find stories like ***No Good Turn Goes Unpunished.***

Contact me on
robyncrye.author@gmail.com

Chapter 1

"You said you would accompany me; you can't back out now."

Kennedy dropped her backpack on the floor as she glared at her sister.

"I know I said I'd go, but I hate hiking, and with your backpack filled to the brim, this hike will be well beyond my ability and out of my comfort zone. Maybe you should see if you could join a hiking club, and then you wouldn't have to badger me."

"Claire, today is the first day of the school holidays, and the weather forecaster predicts heatwave conditions later in the week. I wanted your company today."

"I'm sorry, but I'm not prepared to put myself through agony to keep you company. If it's hot for the rest of the week, I'll sit in front of the TV with you, with the air conditioner running. That's more my style."

Kennedy sighed and hoisted her backpack, then slid her phone into her pocket and waved to her sister.

"Wait, Ken, where are you going?"

"My itinerary is on a sheet of paper stuck to the fridge. I should be home before dark."

As she drove to the trailhead, Kennedy could feel the excitement building. Hiking might not be on her sister's wish list, but Kennedy loved the outdoors, and this trail was her favourite. The car park for hikers attempting the track held three other cars, so Kennedy assumed she might encounter other walkers on her outward journey. It was nice to feel part of the walking community, and if she wanted company in the future, it might be wise to see if there was a hiking club. Kennedy gave her equipment a final check before adjusting the straps on her pack, and, with the pack snug against her shoulder blades, she walked to the head of the trail.

Kennedy revelled in the fresh air and lack of people for the first hour. While she enjoyed her job as a teacher, the endless mounds of paperwork that followed each student piled up by the end of the term. Even today, with computers tracking scores, Kennedy still has to input the data before it can be collated and used in report cards. She sipped her drink as she walked, but, realising the time approached midday, Kennedy found a rocky outcrop and settled onto a boulder in the shade. Once she finished her lunch, she looked ruefully at the extra food she had packed for her sister and shrugged. There was enough food for her to eat lunch a second time, and she thought that by the end of the day, she might be grateful for the extra food.

Once she was ready to go, she heard footsteps approaching and looked up to see a group of three people headed her way. She smiled and waved, and they stopped when they reached her. The hikers looked agitated, and Kennedy assumed there was a problem with the track ahead. To her amazement, the hikers were adamant that she not go much further because they had discovered a wild dog, and the vicious snarling and lunging had convinced them not to continue. From the hikers' description, the dog sounded like a German Shepherd, but a dog loose on the trail was unusual. Had the dog and its master become separated? Kennedy thanked the others for their warning and pondered her options. The track would be clear if the dog and its owner were reunited. Kennedy decided to push on, and if she came across the dog, she could retrace her steps and complete the hike another day.

After walking for another hour, Kennedy wished she had asked the other hikers how far up the track the dog was. She was past the halfway mark, and if she had to turn around and go to the beginning of the route, it would be best to make a move now rather than still be on track as night fell. Kennedy hesitated, trying to decide the best option:

continue and hope for the best, or turn around and try another day. After a moment's hesitation, Kennedy chose to push on. Aware that there may be a potential hazard on the track, Kennedy ceased walking in a dream and concentrated on each footfall she made. She was nearing the end of the trail and sighed with relief that the dog that caused the other hikers she met to return to the start must have moved away.

As Kennedy checked her watch for the time, she rounded a bend, and a dog's low, menacing growl stopped her in her tracks. Kennedy's eyes opened wide as the dog crouched, and she knew there was no way she could run from it. A running target to a dog like this was prey, and Kennedy didn't like her chances at fending him off. She looked around cautiously. There was no convenient tree to scale, and the longer she remained, the more danger she was in. Walking backwards away from the dog was unsuccessful, and rather than extending the distance between them, the dog advanced. Kennedy took a deep breath and looked closely at the dog. It was in poor condition; its backbone and ribs protruded, and she could see the collar and a dangling pendant attached to it despite the dirt on its coat. The tag resembled the badge the police wore on their uniforms, and suddenly Kennedy realised this must be the animal the police had lost while trying to apprehend a criminal months ago. She shook her head; if this dog was a police dog, had his training stayed with him? With nothing to lose, Kennedy said, "Sit", and used her hand in the upward sit motion. The dog quivered and then lowered itself into a sitting position.

The volume of the growling decreased, and Kennedy smiled to herself. With luck, she might come out of this situation alive. If the dog knew the sit command, Kennedy hoped he was well-trained enough to follow her subsequent orders. Pointing to the ground, she told the dog to drop, and when he was on his haunches, she instructed him to stay. When it appeared he would remain where she had ordered him to, Kennedy pulled out her phone and punched in triple zero.

"Police, Fire or ambulance?"

"Ah, I need police, but not your ordinary copper; I need someone from the dog squad."

"If you are in danger, I can send the police.'

"I'm not in danger, but there is a dog here, and I think…"

"If you have a dog problem, call your local council, and they will send a ranger. This line is an emergency one; we do not deal with lost or roaming dogs."

"I understand the centre's purpose, but my situation is unique. Do you have a supervisor I could speak to?"

When the line went dead, Kennedy thought the woman had hung up on her, but a man spoke as she considered her next option.

"You seem to be having an issue with the woman who answered the phone, and she has directed her call to me. I assume you are not in danger or need an ambulance, so what seems to be the problem?"

"The issue is that the lady on the other end will not listen to my problem before she offers options. I am at the walking track at Lonsdale Point and have encountered a dog that I am sure is the police dog that went missing a few months ago. I need someone from the dog squad, not a local ranger, to come and collect the dog. He is wearing a police tag and is very poor but not friendly, so the officer will need to be experienced with these dogs. Can you find someone from the dog squad to come and collect him?"

"Ah, I see why our receptionist was having trouble; this is an unusual case. Let me check your phone number, and I will call you back. Are you safe with the dog?"

"Yes, he is well trained, so I have him in the drop position and have told him to stay."

"I will call you back shortly."

Once Kennedy hung up, she wondered how much leeway the dog would give her when it came to moving around. She wanted to remove her backpack and get a water bottle, but didn't want to provoke the dog. Cautiously, keeping her eyes peeled, Kennedy slid the straps of her pack and moved it to rest on her lap. The dog's only reaction was to flick an ear towards her, but apart from that, he sat quietly. As she unscrewed the lid, the dog slid on its belly closer to her, and Kennedy realised that the dog was eyeing the water. Using her empty lunch box, Kennedy emptied the water bottle's contents into the container and slid closer to the dog. What to do now? The dog couldn't drink flat on the ground, but Kennedy was loath to release him from his prone position. Grimacing and hoping for the best, Kennedy said, " Come." After hesitating, the dog moved towards her, and she held out the water container. Thirst won out over caution, and the dog gulped the contents of Kennedy's bottle before edging back and watching her. When she gave him the down command, he obliged, and Kennedy wondered how long the triple-zero operator might be.

When her phone rang, she and the dog flinched, and before answering, Kennedy gave the dog the "stay" command. She didn't want the phone to spook him, and she doubted he could live in the wild much longer before starvation killed him. The good news was that the operator had found a dog squad member nearby who would be with her in 15 minutes.

"Well, mate, what about having a sandwich while we wait?"

Searching in her bag, she removed Claire's sandwich and offered it to the dog. He crawled forward and whined.

"Here you go; you can have this."

But despite wanting the food, Kennedy's companion refused to eat.

"Damn, you have to hear a code word before you eat and try as I might. I'm sure I won't be able to find the right word."

Kennedy tried using "okay," "righto," and "eat," but before she could think of anything else, a male voice said, "Waterloo."

The dog devoured the sandwich in one gulp and looked at Kennedy, asking for more. Without looking over her shoulder, Kennedy pulled out the second sandwich and held it in her hand.

When she said "Waterloo", the dog took it from her hand. Kennedy laughed and turned to see who had given her the right word.

"Thanks for that. I felt awful offering the food before I realised you would have a code word."

Rising to her feet, Kennedy held out her hand and looked at the voice's owner for the first time. The man was tall and stocky, although Kennedy wasn't sure if that was his natural physique or if the police-issue overalls made him look that way. He had dark hair and was handsome in a wholesome way; he would never walk the catwalks or star on the front of a magazine, but he wouldn't frighten children either.

"I'm Kennedy McCann, and I assume this dog is yours, or you know him well. He scared off some other hikers, but I stumbled onto him before I realised he was there. I thought he might take my throat out, but it turned out okay."

The policeman shook her hand. "I'm Ben Foster, and I can't believe you have him practically eating out of your hand."

"That's thanks to whoever trained him; I used the basic commands to make him stop threatening me, and then we bonded over a lunchbox full of water."

The man nodded. "Where is your car?"

Kennedy gave a rueful laugh. "At the other end of the track. I was going to hike to this end, rest and hike back, but at the rate I'm going, it will be dark before I get to the other end."

Ben said, "Come with me to the vet, and you can fill me in as we go. I'll drive you back to your car when we finish."

Chapter 2

Ben tapped his leg and said. "Come."

The dog immediately fell in beside Ben's leg, and he leaned down to pat the dog.

"You sure know how to get yourself into trouble, don't you, buddy?"

As they approached the van, Ben said, "I would generally put him in his crate, but I think I may lay him on the back seat today. He's too malnourished to keep himself steady in the cage."

"Does your dog have a name?"

Ben raised his eyebrows. "What, you think I yell out, 'Hey, you' when I want him?"

"Smart arse. Okay, let me rephrase my question. What is your dog's name? And I guess from your interaction that he is your dog. Am I right?"

"He is my dog, and his name is Duke. I had given up on ever seeing him again, so finding him is a big deal. You could have run off like the other hikers, but you didn't. So, thanks."

"I didn't run because he looked pretty fierce, and I thought running might convince him I was prey."

Kennedy told Ben that she and Duke reached an amicable arrangement: he didn't attack her, and she provided him with water and food. Ben pulled into the parking lot in front of an old-fashioned brick building.

"Is this where you lock me in the dungeon?"

Ben grinned. "Sure, with chains around your ankles and cuffs on your wrists."

Ben lifted Duke from the back seat and carried him towards the breezeway before pushing the door and entering a hallway. The old-fashioned linoleum was cracked and stained, and Kennedy shook her head in dismay. Ben saw the movement and said, "The police hierarchy realise the value of the dogs, but don't fund anything that doesn't benefit them. Nobody except the handlers sees this area, so why bother making it pretty? It's a bone of contention amongst the squad, but they tell us funds are tight, and dogs don't care about aesthetics."

Ben pushed another door, and they entered an examination room. A middle-aged man entered the room and zeroed in on the patient. As he ran his eye over the dog, he shook his head.

"Well, isn't this one for the books? After two months, who thought we'd see this boy again? He's emaciated, but he must have hunted something to eat, or he'd be dead by now."

Ben nodded. "Yeah, that was my thought. Doc, this is Kennedy, and she is the brave lady who calmed Duke enough to give him water and offer him food, which he refused to eat."

The vet raised his eyes. "Thank you for saving our boy, but you must be a dog whisperer if you didn't get eaten alive when you approached him."

Kennedy laughed. "It was touch and go there for a while."

"Ben, I want to keep him here for a week or two. He's dehydrated and, at a guess, twenty kilos underweight, if not more. I'll start him on a drip and a high-protein diet. He needs to put on a few kilos before I release him, but you might want to put him in the kennels so they can monitor his weight. He'll need three feeds a day and medication before each meal, and unless you intend to take time off, he's better in the kennels."

"I'll give it some thought. Our dog whisperer needs to return to her car, so I'd better do that before her family sends out a search party. Call me if anything changes."

Kennedy followed Ben from the building, her mind racing with possibilities.

"You don't sound thrilled with the idea of Duke going into the kennels."

"He's been gone for nearly two months, and I need him to reconnect with me; that's hard to do if I only manage to visit him between shifts. As a rule, the kennels operate during business hours; however, I suppose I could ask the night assistant to grant me access. However, even then, he would still be in the kennels. I want him at home, but it's not feasible to take months off to nurse him back to health."

"Did I tell you that I'm a school teacher?"

Ben looked curiously at Kennedy.

"Ah, no."

"Well, I am, and I have six weeks' holiday before I have to return. If you want Duke at home, I could feed and medicate him if you trust me to be alone in your house."

"That's a kind offer, but I wouldn't want to impose on you. Holidays are for resting, not nursing a sick dog."

Kennedy shrugged. "The offer is there if you change your mind."

Kennedy collected her backpack from the rear seat of Ben's patrol car. She knew what she wanted to ask Ben, but Kennedy didn't want him to think she was making a move on him. With a shrug, she said,

"Ben, can I have your phone number? I want to check on Duke's progress, if that is alright."

Ben took her phone, typed in his number and name, and then sent himself a text. He smiled. "There, now we have contact details. Give it a few days before you check because I can't imagine there will be much improvement for a few days."

Ben drove away, his mind in turmoil. The return of his dog by an attractive woman was enough to confuse anyone. Should he take Kennedy up on her offer, or would that be asking too much of a stranger? Before deciding, he would run her through the system to see if she had any felony convictions, which would disqualify her; he wasn't giving a convicted felon access to his house. A search on his computer revealed no red flags; Kennedy had a clean record, and he didn't even have any driving infringement notices. It would have been easier if she had convictions because he wouldn't have had a choice. Ben decided he needed to discuss the issue with someone, and the only other person he had met who had met Kennedy was the vet.

The following day, Ben went to the clinic during his lunch break, hoping to find Doctor Simmonds there and have time to chat. When Ben arrived, he heard Doctor Simmonds talking to someone in the consulting room, so he headed back to the recovery cages. Duke wagged his tail when he saw Ben, but was too weak to rise from his bed. Duke was cleaner than when Ben and Kennedy dropped him off, so someone had decided he was strong enough to withstand the rigours of the washstand. Ben wanted to let Duke out of the cage, but the drip attached to one of his feet dissuaded him. He turned when he heard a noise behind him. Doctor Simmons was standing, hands in his pockets, with a frown on his face.

"We washed your bloke yesterday, and I was worried it was too soon, but he came out of it like a champ. Have you decided what to do with him when I release him?"

"That's why I'm here, apart from visiting Duke. You're the only person who has met Kennedy, and I want your opinion. She is a school teacher on a six-week holiday and has offered to nurse Duke at home. If she does, I will spend my off-duty hours with him to build on our connection. I ran her through the system, and she has no convictions or infringement notices, but I am unsure whether letting her into our lives is the best thing I can do. What would you do?"

"I gather you're not happy about the kennels."

"He's been missing for two months; we need to spend time together, and Kennedy's suggestion would give us that time. I would see him between my shifts in the kennels, but not as often as if he were at home."

"It appears you've answered your question. Ask the lassie and see how it goes."

As Ben entered his house, he removed his gun, undid his heavy belt and shrugged off his uniform jacket. With Duke missing for so long, the boss had reassigned Ben to general duties, and even if he spent all day in the car, he needed a shower when he walked in the door. Once he was clean, he searched the fridge for something to eat for dinner, all the while knowing that he was procrastinating. What if Kennedy had made the offer on the spur of the moment and regretted her suggestion? Why would an attractive woman spend her holidays nursing a sick dog? Surely, she had other things to do during her break. Ben dithered about calling Kennedy but eventually decided that if she had made the offer on the spur of the moment and now regretted her suggestion, she could always back out.

Another problem presented itself. After years of training and working towards a promotion, Ben had minimal contact with women who weren't colleagues. How would he deal with an attractive woman in his personal space for weeks or months, depending on Duke's recuperation? Recognising that his options for Duke's recovery were limited, Ben picked up the phone.

Chapter 3

When the phone rang, Kennedy looked at the readout before answering. She was pleased that Ben had kept his word and assumed he was ringing to update her on Duke's condition.

"Hello, Ben. How's your boy?"

"Hi, Kennedy, he's a bit brighter and was pleased to see me today, so that's a start. One of the vet nurses bathed him, so he was clean instead of having a month's worth of dirt on him. Yesterday, when you offered to nurse Duke, was that a knee-jerk reaction or did you mean it?"

"I meant it, but I understand you don't want a stranger in your house."

"Well, can I tell you that I ran you through the system, and you haven't even got a driving infringement? There might be other people who would offer to look after Duke, but even my family are a little afraid of him. He doesn't scare you, so would you consider nursing him at home? Depending on my shifts, I could look after him some days, but other days, you might be there all day."

Kennedy chuckled. "I'm not sure if I admire your security measures or if I should be offended that you put me through your system. Should we meet to work out feed times, medication and anything Doctor Simmonds thinks he needs? I need to know your roster so I can see when you need me and when you can handle the nursing yourself. When did you want to bring Duke home?"

"I'll give Doc another few weeks with him because I'd prefer not to deal with an IV. Can we meet tomorrow to finalise the details? I could buy you dinner to thank you for saving my dog."

"That's unnecessary, but I would enjoy a meal I don't have to cook, so thank you."

"I'm supposed to finish at five o'clock, so do you want me to pick you up or meet you somewhere?"

"I live close, but I'll drive myself if you insist I sit in the back of a police car."

Ben chuckled. "I have a civilian car, and we can use that."

They organised a time for Ben to collect Kennedy and chatted for a few minutes before Kennedy ended the call.

When Claire walked into the room, she raised her eyebrows. "What are you smiling about, Sis?"

"That was Ben. He's decided to let me nurse his dog, so we're having dinner tonight to work out the logistics of the schedule."

"Are you interested in the dog or the man?"

"My primary concern was for Duke, but it doesn't hurt that his handler is nice."

"Nice? That's your appraisal of him?"

"Yeah, but he is nice. He is attractive, but not drop-dead gorgeous, and has a quiet confidence. I'm not sure whether the confidence existed before he became a cop or is a result of it, but he appeals to me either way. I'm looking forward to dinner tonight, and even if nothing comes of it, a night out is always good."

"The police train those dogs to bring criminals to the ground, and nobody seems annoyed if the dog bites the offender. Aren't you frightened he might turn on you?"

"No. If Duke were going to attack, he would have when I came face-to-face with him on the track. And I don't think those dogs attack people randomly; the handler instructs them to tackle crooks. Ben is not frightened of him, nor is the vet, so I hope I become one of his special people."

Ben arrived on time, and without his uniform, he looked different. Today, he wore a pair of dress pants and a long-sleeved shirt, sleeves rolled to his elbows. The shirt's open neck revealed a sprinkle of hair, and Kennedy felt her pulse race. When Kennedy first met Ben, she thought he was bulky, and he was, but his muscles added the extra layer. His exposed forearms confirmed that he was a regular at the gym. Did the police officers have a fitness program they had to follow? Ben made a sound in his throat, and Kennedy's perusal of the man came to an embarrassed halt. The cad grinned at her as her face flushed.

"I was noticing that you look different out of your uniform. Sorry if I was staring."

Ben laughed. "That's okay; you look different in a dress, so we are even in the staring contest. Are you ready to go?"

"Yes, I'll just grab my bag."

The restaurant Ben chose for their meal was a mom-and-pop establishment, and the menu included dishes Kennedy hadn't eaten since her Grandma died.

"Gosh, look at all the traditional dishes. This place might become my favourite eatery."

"Yeah, I get sick of fast food and chicken and chips, so this place is a nice change."

After they made their selections, they chatted about their families and employment. Kennedy was pleased that there were no awkward moments as the conversation flowed.

Ben recounted some funny stories about his time in the academy, and Kennedy reciprocated with stories from the classroom. When Ben called for the check, Kennedy said,

"We haven't discussed what to do with Duke."

"As you are going to be in my house for the next few weeks, I thought we could discuss matters at my place unless you are uncomfortable about that."

"Oh, that makes sense. I'll need a copy of your roster, a key, and the instructions from Doctor Simmonds."

"Yep, and we need a roster of when we take turns nursing Duke."

"When will he be well enough to come home?"

"Doc Simmonds says he's making great improvements with his weight gain, so he thinks in another week or two."

"Can I visit him before he comes home to see if he remembers me? It might be tricky if he thinks I'm an intruder and bails me up in the hallway."

"Sure. I'll ring Doc and see what time suits him. I'll give him your number; he can ring you when he's not busy. Does that suit you?"

"That would be great."

Ben pulled into the driveway of a bungalow-type dwelling. It sprawled amidst a garden of shrubs and natives. Even though there were other houses next door and across the road, Ben's house was set apart from its neighbours. As he approached the house, lights flicked on, illuminating the area. Kennedy wondered if the lights were a security feature or a convenience for navigating in the dark. She knew police officers worked night shifts, so the lights might be necessary depending on when Ben arrived home. Ben unlocked the door and flicked the light on inside; before her lay a fantastic, open area.

"Wow, this is nice."

Ben nodded. "Thanks. When I bought the house, there were small rooms, and I wanted a more open plan. It took a while, but I have it the way I want it now, and I must say I'm pleased with the openness of the rooms. Come to the kitchen, and if we sit at the bar, we can look at my schedule and yours."

An hour later, they had organised the plan to care for Duke, and Ben offered to drive Kennedy home.

"Thanks, Ben. I enjoyed tonight, both the meal and the planning afterwards. I will visit Duke tomorrow, and when Doctor Simmonds decides to send him home, we can implement our plan."

After winding their way through the nearby streets, Ben pulled up outside Kennedy's house. He walked Kennedy to the door, pecked her on the cheek and returned to the car when she went inside.

Chapter 4

The following day, Kennedy visited Duke. The phone call from Doctor Simmonds came as Kennedy was eating a late breakfast, and with nothing planned for the day, she was happy to hear from the Doctor. While on school holidays, Kennedy used the time to recover from the stress of teaching and to prepare programmes for the following year. Even though there was a national curriculum, and the government thoroughly checked students' progress, they were never generous regarding aids to assist learning. Kennedy swore she would be rich if she didn't spend so much on aides and things for the classroom.

Helping Ben care for Duke would eat into her free time, but she relished the challenge of returning the dog to full activity. Kennedy loved dogs, and once she settled the details of her new property, she hoped to have one. Interacting with Duke would give her dog time until she could get a companion. Kennedy knew that when it came to looking after Duke in Ben's house, she would initially feel awkward, but if he trusted her to be alone, she would take that as a compliment. But right now, they weren't there yet. Duke had to gain more weight before Doc Simmonds would allow Ben to take him home.

As Kennedy pushed the door to enter the veterinary practice, she marvelled at the Doctor's work despite the dismal surroundings. When Doctor Simmonds saw her, he held up his hand, his phone clamped in the other hand. Kennedy couldn't help but hear the terse voice and occasional swear words that the Doctor used in response to his caller. Kennedy moved forward when Doctor Simmonds slammed the receiver on the old-fashioned wall unit.

"Ah, have I come at a bad time?"

"No, your enthusiasm for that renegade dog is what I need to restore my good humour. Do you want to come through, and we'll see if he remembers you?"

Doctor Simmonds pushed the door open and walked along the rows of kennels. Duke watched the doctor approach with barely a flicker, but when Kennedy came into view, he stood, his tail wagging frantically.

"I think that confirms he has only fond memories of you. Do you want to get him out?"

Kennedy smiled and nodded, and a few moments later, Duke was sitting next to her, his head in her lap. The Doctor laughed, and Kennedy said, "My sister was concerned that Duke might think I was a criminal and drag me to the ground. When he's like this, you wonder if he was a lap dog in his first life."

"Let me know when you finish visiting, and I'll give you a rundown on his treatment, as Ben tells me you have kindly offered to fit in meals and medication when he can't."

When Duke was tired, Kennedy put him back into the cage, and he settled on the thick mattress that was his bed. Doctor Simmonds told her much the same as Ben did, but she knew not only that Duke was important to Ben, but also that his training was expensive, so losing him because of negligence would not be viewed favourably.

Over the following days, Kennedy organised her activities around visits to Duke. When Ben called her, she assumed it was to discuss Duke's departure date from the kennels, but much to her surprise, Ben asked her to join him at the pub. The dog squad members gathered weekly at a local pub, and Ben wanted to introduce her to them. The story of Duke's rescue was a legend among the squad members, who wanted to meet her. Ben was on duty until five, so they agreed to drive their cars and meet at six. Kennedy wasn't sure how long she wanted to stay, and even though she had met Ben three or four times, she wasn't sure if he was a big drinker, and she had no intention of hanging around or calling a taxi if he wanted to spend the night reminiscing with his mates.

Kennedy arrived at the pub shortly after six, and when she entered, she realised the pub was the local haunt for the district's police. The room was crowded, and after scanning the room with no sign of Ben, she walked past tables of male and female officers until she reached the bar.

"What'll you have, luv?"

"Ah, I'm waiting for someone, so for now, just a Coke, please."

"One Coke coming up. You haven't been here before, have you? I have a good memory and don't recall seeing you here. By the way, I'm Luke."

"Hi, I'm Kennedy. This is my first time here. I've never seen so many cops in one place when it wasn't a riot or a protest."

The barman chuckled and moved along to serve other patrons. Scanning the room again, Kennedy cursed Ben. If he was running late, couldn't he have called? She'd give him until she finished her drink, and she would leave. Kennedy rolled her eyes when a man slid onto the stool beside her. Even in a cop bar, some man had to hit on her.

"Hi, sweetheart, a pretty girl like you shouldn't be sitting at the bar by herself. Why don't you join me at a table, and we could get to know each other?"

Without turning to acknowledge the man, Kennedy said, "No thanks, I'm waiting for someone."

"Your date is a fool if he leaves a pretty thing like you alone when this place crawls with eligible men."

As he spoke, the man edged closer to Kennedy, and when he slung his arm around her shoulders, she shrugged him off.

"Barkeep, order the pretty lady a drink on my tab."

"I don't want a drink paid for by anyone else. What I do want is for you to leave me alone."

Kennedy slid along the bar, and for a moment, she thought she had rid herself of her tormentor when a hand patted her ass, but her butt cheek received a pinch. Without thought, she swung around and punched her tormentor in the nose. The man hit the ground with a thud, blood pouring from his damaged nose. It felt like everyone in the bar took a breath, and then a group of women along the wall stood and cheered. Kennedy shook her hand, trying to alleviate the pain. Before she moved away, the bartender called her name and handed her an ice pack. She grimaced at him and gratefully took the icepack. The cold pack might relieve the swelling, but it did little to ease the ache. The bartender threw a wad of napkins at the injured man, who regained his feet and began to shout.

"Officer Briggs, arrest this woman for assault."

As an embarrassed officer approached, Kennedy gave him a winning smile

"If you intend to arrest me, officer, you had better ask your partner to arrest Mr Handsy there. I believe most people here saw his sexual harassment of me and then his sexual assault."

The officer backed off, embarrassed, with a shrug.

"I'll see you in court, woman. You can't get away with assaulting a police officer. My solicitor will tear you to pieces."

Kennedy looked at the blowhard and shook her head.

"Is that so? Don't forget to tell him you sexually harassed me, and when you wouldn't leave me alone, you sexually assaulted me. I do believe your solicitor, if he has a brain, will tell you that you got off light."

Everyone in the room watched the man stalking out, and Kennedy wanted to sink onto one of the barstools, but the women at the side table urged her to join them. Kennedy looked at the time, and it was half past six. Where the hell was Ben? With a shrug, she approached the women's table, only to be met with high-fives and slaps on the back. Bemused by her reception, Kennedy joined the group when they begged her to sit with them. A petite blonde introduced themselves and filled Kennedy in on their appreciation.

"That sleaze bag is our head of department, and he touches and pinches and stands too close, and he once grabbed Nora's boob. No amount of complaining to HR or our commander results in any action, so tonight, we salute you!"

The women raised their glasses, and Kennedy frowned.

"If you can't get any action from your HR and commander, make an appointment to see Katarina. She says she wants a clean and inclusive police force, so a delegation to her might clean up your workplace."

"That's a brilliant idea. Are you here to meet someone, or did you hope to snag a cop for the night?"

"I was supposed to meet Ben Foster at six o'clock, and I'm okay with him being late, but a text message might be nice."

The blond woman, Jill, said, "Ooh, he's yummy. He's probably worth the wait."

"Ah, here he comes now."

Kennedy looked over her shoulder, and Ben was indeed approaching. He looked flustered, and his hair was mussed as though he had run his fingers through it numerous times. Despite his disarray, Kennedy silently agreed with the woman who said Ben was yummy. When he approached the booth, he said,

"Ladies, thank you for looking after Kennedy."

The women all laughed. The officer named Jill said, "You've got a live one here, Foster. Wait till your mates fill you in; I won't spoil their fun."

Ben quirked an eyebrow at Kennedy, and she blushed under his scrutiny. His eyes scanned the icepack she held on her knuckles, and he frowned.

"Well, there seems to be a story here, and I can't wait to hear it. Kennedy, will you join me at the dog squad's table?"

Kennedy winked at her new female friends and followed Ben to the table closest to the bar. When he introduced her to the men sitting at the table, there were chuckles all around.

The oldest of the group said, "The female cops have to endure that behaviour every day. I can't understand why they don't complain. He got what he deserved tonight, and if you get a lawyer's letter, let us know; we'll go in to bat for you."

"Thanks, I appreciate that. And, by the way, the women said they have complained to HR and the commander, and they pass the behaviour off as that of an old timer who hasn't caught up with modern expectations. That excuse is hogwash because I bet he didn't pinch the butt cheeks of his wife's sisters and friends in the good old days."

Ben had returned with his drink and another Coke for Kennedy as the conversation continued.

"What on earth happened before I arrived?"

Kennedy let the men tell the story and avoided Ben's eyes when they reached the punch line. For a moment, Ben said nothing as he scrutinised Kennedy, and then he started to laugh.

"So you're not going to sack me from helping with Duke?"

"Not a chance, Kennedy, not a chance, but seeing as I wanted to introduce you to my teammates, it seems you've already broken the ice. I'm sorry I was late; you wouldn't have had to endure that lecherous fool if I had been on time."

Turning to his fellow dog squad members, Ben said, "I wanted to introduce Kennedy to you guys because she is the person who found Duke. Without her intelligent handling of him, we might have had to euthanise him while calling the paramedics for Kennedy."

As she told her story, the officers stared in disbelief as she recounted how she calmed the agitated dog and called for help. She explained what happened when she called triple zero and how desperate Duke was to eat the sandwich, but because she didn't know the code word, he resisted. The man Ben introduced as the commander said,

"I'm stunned but relieved. The uproar about police dogs would have been enormous had you been injured, and the money you have saved the department is substantial because training our dogs is not cheap. You've given Ben back his partner; when he's fit, they can recommence working in our unit."

The conversation flowed until Kennedy's rumbly tummy announced her need for food. Blushing, she told Ben she needed to leave, but he insisted on buying her a meal, so they left to find an open eatery. As they walked through the tables to the entrance, the lady officers stopped her. Kayla, the tallest of the group, said, "Kennedy, we would love you to join us one night soon. Can I have your number, and I'll call you?" Once the women exchanged numbers, Kennedy and Ben headed out into the street to hunt for a place to eat.

Kennedy and Ben settled on the Thai restaurant halfway down the street. Kennedy suddenly felt shy, but Ben was so easy to talk to, and with his understanding and interest in current affairs and the world in general, Kennedy felt herself relaxing. The night, which had started badly, improved with her conversations with the officers Kennedy met, and she was happy that she had allowed Ben to introduce her to his colleagues. Even though they had their own cars, Ben insisted on following Kennedy home. His insistence touched Kennedy, and she drove cautiously through the traffic until she reached her house. When she parked in the driveway, she realised Ben had alighted from his vehicle. As he approached her, Kennedy laughed.

"Are you going to book me for a driving infringement, Officer Foster?"

Ben shook his head, and an amused expression crossed his face.

"I'm going to walk you to your door and wait until you are safely inside before I go home. I can't have you mugged on the street; Duke would never forgive me."

Ben followed Kennedy the short distance to her door and waited while he unlocked it.

"Thanks for introducing me to your team. Despite the start, I had a good time."

Ben looks shame-faced. "Did I ever apologise for being late? I was on my way when I came across a lady in a broken-down car. I stayed with her until the tow truck arrived, which made me late for our meeting. I'm sorry."

"I can hardly be cross, seeing as you were being a white knight, but a phone call would have been good."

Ben kissed Kennedy on the cheek and stepped away, waiting for her to enter her house. Once she was inside with the door locked, she heard Ben walk away. When Kennedy peeked out the window, she watched as he climbed into his car and drove away. When Kennedy started her holidays two weeks ago, she would have scoffed if someone had suggested she would meet a handsome man who would tweak her slumbering libido. Never in her wildest dreams would she have guessed that a hike on the trail would result in a life-changing occurrence, but here she was, ready to nurse the dog of a sexy police officer. The cheek kiss showed affection, but could it go further? Kennedy decided to take each day as it came.

Chapter 5

Ben's phone call alerted Kennedy that Doctor Simmonds was releasing Duke from the clinic, and that their tag-teaming to keep him fed and medicated would start the next day. As per their agreement, Ben would feed Duke before he went to work, and Kennedy would arrive around eleven to keep him company until she fed him at twelve. The afternoon arrangements were fluid because if something delayed Ben, it would disrupt Duke's medication and feeding schedule, so Kennedy would remain until Ben returned home. Kennedy didn't mind this arrangement because it allowed her plenty of time to catch up on her reading. The length of the agreement depended on how long it took for Duke to recover. Still, if it lasted until Christmas, Kennedy could change her reading books for her planning documents and focus solely on the curriculum for the upcoming year.

The following day, letting herself into Ben's home felt strange, but Kennedy pushed away her awkwardness and walked through the house to the kitchen. After laying her bag and a stack of books on the counter, Kennedy smiled as she noticed Ben's note. The note contained all the instructions regarding Duke's care, and considering she had heard the instructions from Doctor Simmonds and Ben, the letter seemed redundant, but Kennedy knew that the men were concerned about the arrangement's success, so she would give them a leave pass this time. As she walked towards the back porch, the thumping of a tail made Kennedy smile, and she squatted next to Duke's bed, where he lay reclined on his side. Kennedy fussed over Duke before checking his water and retrieving her reading material. Duke was supposed to remain quiet, and except for toilet breaks, Kennedy had to encourage him to stay on his bed.

The day passed quickly, with Kennedy and Duke keeping each other company. After Kennedy fed and medicated Duke, she walked him a short distance to encourage him to do his business, and then the two returned to the porch. When her phone rang, and the call was from Ben, Kennedy knew he would be home soon, so after chatting with him, she packed her books and headed home. The first week with Ben on day duty passed uneventfully, and while Kennedy missed seeing him, she knew that despite the cheek kiss, Ben most likely felt nothing for her except gratitude. The less she saw him, the easier it would be to ignore the attraction she felt for him.

Ben had one more day on his current roster, but when his finishing time arrived, Kennedy hadn't heard from him. She would wait another half an hour, and if she hadn't heard from him, she would feed and medicate Duke and stay until he either rang or returned. Kennedy settled on the couch and was engrossed in the program when she heard the garage door open and a car drive in. When Ben emerged from the laundry, where the door connected to the garage, he looked tired and cross, but as he was carrying two pizzas, Kennedy decided to discuss his late arrival and his failure to contact her until later.

"Hi, Ben. Have you had a tough day?"

Ben slid the pizzas into the warming drawer and grimaced.

"Give me a minute to lock up my gun and shower. I won't be long."

Kennedy returned to the show she was watching, but the interruption disrupted her train of thought, so she switched off the set and went into the kitchen to set out plates and napkins. True to his word, Ben entered the kitchen ten minutes later.

"Where do you want to eat?"

Ben opened the fridge and held up a can of cola towards Kennedy. When she nodded, he placed the pizza boxes on the countertop using oven mitts. Once he dished three slices each, he returned the pizzas to the warming drawer and said, "Will you think me uncouth if I say I want to eat in the lounge room? I've had a bitch of a day, and I can't get up the energy to pretend I'm posh."

Kennedy laughed. "Have you noticed we are eating takeaway, although you put the slices on a plate rather than eating out of the box? I don't think we could make this posh unless you poured the drinks into crystal goblets, and we had linen napkins to wipe up our spills. Do you want to talk about your day, or would you rather hear about my exciting day?"

Ben raised his eyebrows. "You had an exciting day? Do tell."

"Duke and I hung out all day with infrequent walks across the lawn for toileting."

Ben shook his head. "I'm not sure how you'll cope with such a jam-packed and exciting programme."

Kennedy rolled her eyes. "Okay, hotshot, tell me what you did."

"The guys and I did a drug raid, and it amazes me that people are surprised when we arrive with a warrant. They had the whole damn house set up as a drug lab with hydroponic rooms and drying racks. The electricity was through the roof, and the neighbours complained about the smell. It was a no-brainer."

"Well, you won that competition; it sounds like you had a much more exciting day than Duke and I did."

"I owe you an apology."

"Well, if you apologise, not just tell me you owe me one; I will know whether or not I'm prepared to accept your admission of guilt."

"I'm sorry for not ringing to let you know I would be late. I left work on time, but as I drove home, I came across a broken-down car with a distraught woman standing nearby. She had a distressed baby in a car seat, and no one else had stopped to help. She said the battery on her phone was flat, and she had a flat tyre, but knew there was no spare tyre because her boyfriend had removed it when he needed the space in the boot and hadn't replaced it. When I suggested calling her boyfriend, she said he wouldn't come to pick her up, and when I suggested a tow truck, she wept about the difficulty of paying the bill."

"What did you do?"

"I called a tow truck and paid the driver before he hooked up the car; then I drove her and the baby home. Hopefully, the boyfriend can organise the tyre tomorrow."

Kennedy leaned over and kissed Ben on the cheek.

"You, Ben Foster, are a genuinely lovely guy. I can't think of anyone I know who would go to that much trouble for a stranger. Oh, and by the way, I accept your apology."

Ben grinned. "Good, I'd hate to jeopardise our arrangement this early on in the piece. While I'm in a grovelling mood, can you sit with Duke on Sunday? My family have lunch on Sunday each week, and I've missed the last few because of my shifts, although that's always a good excuse for my absence."

"Sure, I can do that."

"Will you have dinner with me on Saturday night? It will be nice to eat something other than take-out, which, unfortunately, is my go-to food."

Chapter 6

Claire watched with amusement as Kennedy tried on outfit after outfit. Kennedy glared at her sister, "You could at least give me some help here."

"I don't think I've ever seen you so flustered by a date night. I have to meet this guy; he must be special. Wear your skinny jeans and that lacy top with a jacket."

Kennedy pulled out the clothes her sister suggested, and they looked fine. She topped the outfit with her boots, clipped in her jangly earrings and called it done.

"I'm not even sure this is a date. It might be him saying thank you for staying late the other night. I'm so confused."

"Whether it's a date or not, the outfit looks great."

When Ben arrived, he had a small posy of flowers, and as Kennedy placed them in water, she grinned to herself. The flowers confirmed that this was a date, and she hoped that this night together would be the first of many. Ben had chosen an Italian restaurant, and as the waitress seated them, he said, "I didn't ask if you like Italian. Is it too late to ask? I didn't want to go to a place we could ring for take-out, and I never thought to ask."

"Italian is great, Ben, and I like your choice because Thai or Chinese would feel like take-out even if we ate in a restaurant."

As they tucked into their food, Kennedy was surprised that she and Ben never ran out of things to talk about. Their association began a month ago, but she felt she had known him forever. The more time Kennedy spent with him, the more she realised she wanted more than friendship with Ben. He interested her, intrigued her and attracted her more than any man she had met in recent years. At Claire's insistence, Kennedy had dated briefly, but blind dates organised by friends who swore they knew the right man for her were a trial she refused to participate in after her first failed dates. Kennedy's work kept her busy, and she felt no need for male company, so her attraction to Ben surprised her.

The drive to her house was quiet; neither Kennedy nor Ben wished to break their companionable silence. When Ben stopped in front of her home, he alighted from the car and walked to the passenger side to open the door for Kennedy.

"Let me walk you to the door."

As Kennedy removed her keys from her bag, Ben said, " I have a dilemma."

Kennedy turned to face her dinner partner.

"Do you want to share with me?"

Ben ran his hand over his chin, the scuff on his face bristling as his hand moved.

"I want to kiss you, but I don't want you to get angry and stop nursing Duke."

Kennedy smiled. "I can solve your dilemma for you. Why don't you kiss me, and then you can see if I get angry?"

Ben cupped her face, and his lips whispered across Kennedy's lips. When he stepped back, Kennedy raised her eyebrow. "If that's the best you can do, I will get angry. Do you want to try that again?"

The second kiss made Kennedy lose awareness of their location, and she gripped Ben's forearms to anchor herself. He slid his hands into her hair and tilted her head slightly to give him better access. A groan rumbled in Kennedy's throat as Ben worshipped her lips with his mouth, teeth and tongue. When he stepped away the second time, Kennedy fought for awareness.

"Was that enough to stop you from being angry?"

"I might have to get angry if you don't do that often enough."

Ben pulled Kennedy into his arms.

"I have wanted to kiss you since I saw you sitting on the ground, grieving about Duke's refusal to take the food. If Duke had accosted the scared people, I can see the outcome wouldn't have been happy, and then every handler with a dog would have had to justify using dangerous dogs as part of law enforcement. Duke's head resting in your lap brought tears to my eyes, and I knew then you were special. Everything you have done for Duke and me only confirms my opinion."

Kennedy blushed at his effusive compliments, and she kissed him on the cheek and said goodnight. While she could have stood on the step and kissed him again, she wasn't happy to provide entertainment for her neighbours.

Ben hugged and kissed Kennedy as she arrived at his house on Sunday. When the kiss became heated, Ben considered skipping the family dinner to spend the day with Kennedy, but having committed to attending, he regretfully left the house. Today was the day his family had a meal together, and Ben felt obliged to be there because he had the day off. Ben wanted to tell his family that Kennedy had found Duke and that Duke was recovering. His family might make appreciative noises, but Ben knew they were all afraid of his dog and wouldn't be as excited as he was. Still, he wanted to share.

When Ben opened the wire door to let himself into the house, the noise from the kitchen and the family room alerted him that this family dinner included their next-door neighbours. Ben suddenly remembered why he avoided these get-togethers. His Mother and best friend, Alison Davidson, had always wanted Ben to marry Cherise Davidson. Despite having no chemistry, Ben succumbed to pressure and dated the woman a few years ago. After six dates, he ended their association. When they were children, their mothers pushed them to play with each other, and as a woman, she was still self-absorbed and high-maintenance. Her tantrums and pouting were a daily occurrence, and with a high-stress job, he didn't need more aggravation in his private life. The issue was that his Mother, Alison Davidson and Cherise thought the marriage was a foregone conclusion, and Ben had caught Cherise introducing herself to strangers as his fiancée.

Entering the kitchen, Ben greeted the woman, left them to their preparation and searched for the other men. The other husbands and boyfriends sat glued to the television, a soccer game enthralling them. They took time out to greet him, and when his mother called to say that the meal was ready, they groaned in unison. The women were seated at the table when the men dragged themselves away from the game. The vacant spot beside Cherise made Ben clench his teeth, but he slid into the seat, barely acknowledging the woman.

Once everyone had served their meals, the conversation in the room picked up. Cherise attempted to engage Ben in conversation, but he replied in monosyllables and turned to his brother to chat. His Mother thwarted his plan to avoid a discussion with his supposed fiancée by introducing the subject he did not want to discuss.

"Ben, dear, it's been some time since you joined us. We have all missed you, especially Cherise. It would be best if you were more respectful of your future wife."

Ben placed his cutlery on his plate and glared at his Mother.

"As you know, my job involves shift and night work. I can't drop everything to attend a family dinner. And if you want me to stay away from these events permanently, keep on with your ridiculous plan for Cherise and me to marry. When I marry, the woman will be of my choosing. I came because I wanted to share some good news, although I doubt most people at this table will share in my joy."

Cherise clapped her hands. "Goodie, you have quit the police force and will join my Father in his business."

The table erupted with congratulations and exclamations, and when the joy died, he stared incredulously at his family.

"It astounds me that Cherise's uninformed comment could cause so much joy. Do you believe I would share my plans with her? No, I am not quitting. The news I wanted to share, which gives me great joy, is that a trailwalker has found Duke. He was emaciated, and Doctor Simmonds had him in the clinic for a few weeks, and now he is home building up his strength."

Gabe clapped him on the back. "I must confess that your dog scares the dickens out of me, but I know how distressed you were when he went missing, so I'm happy for you. How did a trail walker come across your dog and not get mauled?"

Ben noticed that no one else had commented, but he told Gabe how Kennedy had found Duke. His brother-in-law, Mark, said, "Blimey mate, she must have balls. Those dogs in flight are terrifying."

"She was both courageous and sensible. Kennedy's helping me medicate and feed him because we have to treat him thrice daily until he gains a target weight, and my dog loves her, so they get to hang out every day."

Cherise screwed her nose up. "So, a random woman found your dog, and when he's fit, you will return to being a dog handler instead of an officer in a vehicle. I can't fathom why you would prefer playing with dogs to expanding your promotional opportunities. If you won't work with my Father, why become a cop? The uniform might be attractive, but the job is little better than a jail warden, and heaven knows that would be a dead-end job."

Before Ben could comment, his Mother said, "Dear, you must think of your future. Can you provide for a wife and child? It's not too much to expect that your occupation can support Cherise and your children."

Ben rose from his seat. "Father, Mr Davidson, perhaps you can explain to your wives that I will not now, or ever, marry Cherise. If Gabe tells the truth, he will back me up when I say that, when we were children, being forced to play with a spoiled girl who threw tantrums when she didn't get her way was never our choice. From what I see each time I come for dinner, it appears that Cherise hasn't changed, and our

Mothers are still pandering to her, so her tantrums continue. I wanted to share my good news with you, but I doubt you even heard what I said. Thanks, Gabe and Mark, for hearing my news and understanding how important that was to me."

Ben walked away, vowing he would never share a meal with his family when the Davidsons were present. Andy Foster, Ben's Father, broke the stunned silence.

"Beth, if you wish to lose your son, you are going about it the right way. He has repeatedly clarified his opinion on your marriage plans, yet you persist in bringing up the subject. You must decide: do you value your friendship above your concern for your son, or does your son come first? The plan to marry Ben to Cherise might have been a wonderful dream, but you are dealing with an independent man, not a boy you can bully."

Gabe said, "Amen to that."

Chapter 7

Ben arrived home in a foul mood, and Kennedy's note on the bench increased his temper. Had she said she was going home after feeding Duke? Ben looked at the time and realised that the torturous meal with his family had gone on for hours, and it was unreasonable to expect Kennedy to be at his beck and call. After all, she had her own life and a sister close by. A whining noise reminded him that Duke needed to be medicated and fed, so after changing into sweats and a T-shirt, he gathered the necessary supplies and went outside to tend to his canine companion and encourage him to walk around the yard.

At home, Kennedy completed her household tasks and began to unpack more boxes. Before starting to nurse Duke, Kennedy had moved into her newly purchased home. She had a list of improvements she needed to implement, but she was happy to be a homeowner. Living with her sister was fun for a while, but as time went on, they began to annoy each other, making her own home a great solution.

As she unpacked, Kennedy's thoughts drifted to Ben. The meal with his family sounded like a trial, but she wasn't sure what the issue was. Did he clash with his parents, or didn't see eye to eye with his siblings? Kennedy realised that while she spent extended periods at Ben's house, she knew little about him outside his job. Ben's day shifts finished at the end of the week, and Kennedy decided she would attempt to convince him to share some things about himself before they saw less of each other during his night shifts.

When Ben opened the door, a tantalising aroma greeted him. Unholstering his gun, Ben walked towards the kitchen, where he found Kennedy dancing to the music from her headphones while she stirred the contents of a pot. Sensing movement behind her, Kennedy swung around and let out a scream. Ben realised he still had his gun in his hand, even though it was facing the ground and held close to his leg, and that Kennedy was startled. With one hand resting against her pounding heart, Kennedy removed the headset.

"Blimey, Ben, you scared the daylights out of me. What's with the gun?"

"Sorry, I smelled something delicious when I unholstered my gun, and I decided to investigate. Give me a minute to lock up my weapon and have a shower. I won't be long."

Fifteen minutes later, Ben joined Kennedy at the bench in the kitchen. The stew she had prepared disappeared from Ben's plate quickly, and while Kennedy ate her meal, Ben dished seconds. Kennedy watched Ben eat with amusement, making appreciative noises.

"Ken, this is so good. Most of my meals are take-out, and although I can cook some simple things, it's not much fun cooking for a solo diner."

"I'm glad you appreciate my efforts, but the food is a bribe. I want to know about your family dynamic and how the lunch went with your family."

Ben grimaced. "Ah, where do I start?"

Ben told Kennedy about the family from next door's constant presence and his Mother's expectation that he should marry Cherise.

"When we were kids, Gabe and I had to include her in our games because our Mothers are best friends. If we didn't play the games Cherise wanted, she would cry and tell our Mothers that we were being mean. Once we got a little older, we didn't want to pander to Cherise any longer, so we played cricket, even though standing in the sun for hours wasn't much fun. We had to practise two nights a week, and the game took up most of the weekend, so there was no time for our Mothers to insist we play with the girl. We thought we were brilliant, but when the cricket season finished, we had to find another sport, so we played soccer. Neither Gabe nor I were a terrific sportsman, but getting out of playing with that spoiled brat made us feel fantastic. The problem is that our Mothers think we will eventually get married. A few years ago, I humoured them, thinking they would relent if I had a few dates with Cherise that didn't work. We went out six times; she is as entitled and spoiled as a child could be. She is high maintenance with a side of hysterics, and I don't need that with my job. When I told her I had applied to the police academy, she screamed that I had to choose between her and the force. What a laughable ultimatum!"

"So, what happened on Sunday?"

"My Mother invited the neighbours, and she and Mrs Davidson kept referencing our wedding. When I told them about Duke, Gabe and Mark were the only two who could see how important it was to me. I left shortly after and will not attend another dinner when my Mother invites the Davidsons. I'm sick of the hassling about Cherise. I asked my Father and Mr Davidson to explain my refusal to their wives, but I don't know if they will or how successful it will be."

Kennedy sat silently, an amazed expression on her face.

"Wow, hasn't anyone told your Mother and her friend that it isn't the eighteen hundreds? Arranged marriages went out of fashion centuries ago. What does Cherise have to say? Surely, she can't be oblivious to your reluctance to the arrangement. Why would a woman want a husband who married her because he was forced?"

"I keep hoping the next dinner will improve, but they never do."

As they loaded the dishwasher, Kennedy pondered what Ben had said about his family. If they were to have a relationship, she imagined there would be a lot of pushback from the family and the neighbours. Should she rethink her hope that Ben wanted more than an occasional kiss and a hearty meal? Kennedy would need to give the information Ben had shared careful consideration. She was not getting involved in a family dispute.

Ben watched Kennedy as they loaded the dishwasher. She had gone quiet since his revelation regarding his family and Cherise, and he could almost hear her thinking. He liked Kennedy, and even though they arranged for Kennedy to nurse Duke for his convenience, he had wanted more from her from their first encounter. Ben cursed himself for telling her everything about his family and their delusional objectives. Trying to lighten the mood, Ben pulled two drinks from the fridge and convinced Kennedy to join him on the couch.

"Tell me about your family. I know you have a sister because you mentioned her, but where are your parents? Do you have any other siblings?"

Kennedy nodded. "I have two siblings. You've heard me talk about Claire, but I've a brother who is in the army, so we don't see him very often. Mum and Dad moved to a retirement village in Wallan, and since then, Claire and I have visited every few months. However, they are so busy with their new friends and hobbies that it becomes tricky to organise a time that suits us all. I talk to them on the phone once a week, so we catch up that way."

Kennedy's earlier troubled expression had dissipated as she spoke of her family, and Ben warned himself not to discuss his family again unless Kennedy specifically asked.

Pulling Kennedy into his arms, Ben cupped her face and kissed her. Kissing Kennedy made Ben yearn for much more, but he would go slow for now. Kennedy responded to his kisses with a soft moan, and when his lips slid down to her neck, she slid onto his lap. With her hands wrapped around his neck and her body pressed against his, Ben was fast losing the battle of taking things slowly.

"Kennedy, if we don't stop now, I won't be able to stop. If you don't want to end up in my bed, now would be a good time to slide off my lap."

In response, Kennedy shifted so that she was straddling Ben, and his tortured groan told her all she needed to know. As she ground her wet centre against his erection, she hoped that he would fix the ache inside her and take her to his bed. Ben broke their embrace and shifted Kennedy from his lap. The thought of rejection stung, but it disappeared when Ben slung her over his shoulder and walked towards his bedroom. Kennedy laughed, and, realising that she was tantalisingly close to Ben's tight backside, she slapped him lightly. When he tossed her on the bed, he followed he down onto the mattress before resuming his exploration of her neck with his lips. Kennedy groaned and slid her hands under his shirt, her hands running across his firm stomach muscles. She felt his muscles flex as her hands wandered, and when he yanked his shirt over his head, she had unfettered access to his toned body.

"Ken, stop behaving like an octopus and let me remove your shirt."

With giggles and curses, Ben removed Kennedy's shirt and bra.

"God, you're even more gorgeous with your shirt off than when you're dressed."

As Ben lavished attention on Kennedy's breasts, she explored his body, finally sliding her hands under the band of his pants. Ben's groan of appreciation encouraged Kennedy, and she slid the pants down, tapping him on the bum when she needed his cooperation to slide them down further. Kennedy knew that whatever happened between them after Duke's recovery, she would always feel deeply attracted to this decent, honourable man.

Chapter 8

Ben's night shift changed their routine. Kennedy arrived at lunchtime to feed and medicate Duke, and she remained until Ben rose in the late afternoon. Most nights, they ate at home and spent time together, both in bed and out. Kennedy knew that with every interaction she had with Ben, her feelings for him deepened. She hoped Ben saw her as more than a friend with benefits, but how did she ask?

As his night shift approached, Ben's boss called him to start early as they had a hostage situation playing out, and he needed more bodies on the ground. Ben explained that as Christmas approached, they had more and more domestic violence calls. People didn't call Christmas the silly season for nothing. Kennedy agreed to stay to keep Duke company, and today, she decided to walk him out in the street. His weight gain was encouraging, but his fitness needed to improve before Ben could use him on activations. Duke walked well on the lead for Kennedy, in stark contrast to his behaviour when working to bring down a felon. When she reached the park, Kennedy turned to return home when a man approached her. Duke tensed beside her.

"Nice dog."

The man stretched his hand to pat Duke, and Kennedy wondered at his intelligence. The closer the man got to Kennedy, the lower Duke's growl got. Kennedy drew Duke closer and shook her head.

"Don't touch! Back off! Why would you think patting a strange dog is appropriate without checking with the owner? My dog is saying not to touch, so hear his warning."

The man gave Kennedy a disgusted look, but he did move back.

"Why would you bring a dangerous dog into the park? You should muzzle the mutt if it's dangerous."

"You should learn to ask the owner before patting a dog on a leash. My dog doesn't need a muzzle; you need to act with thought and consideration."

By the time Kennedy returned home, she was both angry and frustrated. The man's rude and forward behaviour had her rethinking the places she took Duke. As long as people didn't approach Duke, he remained calm and respectful. However, Kennedy was unsure whether Duke distrusted the man or if his behaviour would have been the same regardless of who approached him; she would ask Ben about this. However, she doubted he went out in public with Duke when he wasn't working. Kennedy fed Duke his last meal of the day and wondered when Ben would return, considering his early start. Would there be coverage of the hostage stand-off on the news? Kennedy decided to watch the local telecast, but surely the police had resolved the incident by then. The news reporter described the incident as it unfolded, and Kennedy became worried about the officers on the scene, particularly Ben. The more information the reporter gathered, the more concerned Kennedy became, and eventually, she turned off the television. No good could come of panicking while watching the telecast. Looking for something to keep her busy, Kennedy decided to make a meal she could heat up when Ben returned.

A noise woke Kennedy from a deep sleep. She had given up on waiting for Ben, and she and Duke settled comfortably in the lounge room, but at the noise at the door, Duke sat up as Kennedy dragged herself off the couch. When Ben entered the house, Kennedy felt her heart slam against her ribs at the picture her boyfriend presented. Ben's shoulders slumped, and tension showed on his face. The most disturbing feature was the dead look in his eyes, and Kennedy didn't hesitate to offer her arms for comfort. Ben wrapped his arms around Kennedy and hung on tight. She was at a loss to know what to do, so she stepped back and, gathering his keys, directed him to his gun locker, but he was incapable of functioning, so Kennedy removed his gun from its holster and locked it in the safe. He sighed when she unfastened his utility belt and obediently followed Kennedy to the bathroom. As she stripped him, there was nothing sexual about the action; it was more like stripping a child. Kennedy moved Ben under the hot stream of water while she undressed. Following Ben into the shower, she washed him, and when he pulled her close, she held him while he cried. Whatever happened in that hostage incident had shattered Ben, and all Kennedy could do was treat him gently and hope his resilience would eventually return.

Tucked up in bed, Ben wouldn't release Kennedy, so she climbed in with him, and he wrapped his arms around her. When his breath became steady, and she knew he was asleep, she let her emotions pour out. Tears filled her eyes as she grieved for Ben; his heartache and distress would not be easily repaired.

Ben was still asleep when Kennedy heard Duke whimper. Rising carefully, Kennedy left the room and smiled as Duke greeted her. When she opened the door for him to walk on the lawn and relieve himself, Kennedy prepared his meal and measured the medication. She made a mental note to call Doctor Simmonds to check if Duke needed another prescription for the medicine or if he had finished with the tonic and antibiotic. Not willing to disturb Ben, Kennedy showered in the guest bathroom and dressed in fresh clothes. She did a load of washing and considered her options when Ben appeared.

"How are you this morning?"

"Embarrassed, confused, angry and heartsick."

"Do you want to eat while we discuss that sentence?"

"Sure."

Kennedy cracked eggs into the frypan and slid bacon onto baking paper in an oven tray. She poured Ben a mug of coffee and returned to her task. When she plated the meal, she placed her cup of tea and a bowl of cereal on the table. When Ben cleared his plate, Kennedy said,

"Tell me why you are embarrassed."

Ben frowned. "I don't remember what happened after I left work. I don't know how I got home or ended up in bed. But I do remember crying like a baby, and that you were there. Even though I'm embarrassed at blubbering like a baby, I'm still angry and heartsick."

"Let me fill you in, and then we can address your concerns."

Ben watched Kennedy closely as she recounted the events of the previous night. It heartened him when he could see no disgust or embarrassment as she retold the night's events. When she finished her recount, she said, "I've always hated that macho bullshit about real men don't cry. Last night, you had endured a horrific incident, and if crying helps relieve some of the tension, then I'm all for it. I can't help with the anger, but you should see a counsellor. Yes, maybe they debriefed you last night, but throughout your career, you will encounter other incidents that have a huge impact. You can pretend to be macho and try to push this incident deep into your subconscious, and your career will last about five years. If you are in for the long run, you need to take care of your mental health."

Kennedy walked to where Ben sat, stepped between his outspread legs and wrapped her arms around him.

"I feel honoured that you let me help you last night."

Ben cupped her jaw and placed the softest of kisses on her lips. Desperation replaced restraint, and Ben slid his hands into Kennedy's hair and tilted her head for better access. Kennedy slid her arms around his neck, but when Ben stood, she slid her hands to grab his arms and squealed when he spun her and placed her on the bench. When he tapped her legs, she opened them, and Ben moved to stand between her knees. Ben's desperation morphed into passion, and Ben took her on the bench, his eyes blazing and his movements jerky. Their interaction was brief, and although Kennedy didn't climax, she felt only concern and grief for her troubled boyfriend. Ben rested his forehead on hers.

"I'm sorry, that was selfish of me."

Kennedy winked at Ben.

"Don't worry about it. I will punish you later."

She grinned and said, "You'd better check your firearm. It's in your locker, but I didn't know if there was a safety or anything, and I figured I'd shoot myself if I messed around with it."

Ben gave a weak grin. "I might have to teach you about guns. We could spend some time at the shooting range."

They put the subject of the hostage siege to bed, but when Kennedy went online to check the reports, she realised why Ben was so upset. A desperate call from a woman galvanised the police response, but her husband killed her before they arrived. The negotiator spent a day and a half trying to convince the man to release the children, but when a high-pitched scream sounded, the officers went in. The man slit the throats of his two sons and the baby strapped in the highchair before the officers killed him with multiple rounds. No amount of debriefing could make the details of the massacre disappear, and Kennedy was even more determined to have Ben see a counsellor.

Chapter 9

Kennedy wrung her hands in her lap. Meeting Ben's family was daunting, but as their relationship solidified, he wanted his family to meet her. Ben assured her that he had made it clear to his Mother that he wouldn't attend if she invited the Davidsons, and while Mrs Foster scoffed, she finally agreed. When Ben pulled into the driveway, he saw his sister's SUV and Gabe's ute. As they walked towards the front door, Ben took Kennedy's hand, his gentle squeeze conveying his support. When the front door opened, his Mother greeted them with a tight smile.

"It's nice to see you made it, Ben."

"Since you agreed to my conditions, refusing would have been churlish. Let me introduce Kennedy; it was her intervention that saved Duke."

Mrs Foster sniffed. "I'm not sure her intervention was for the best, but time will tell."

It didn't go unnoticed that Mrs Foster did not greet Kennedy, and her anxiety at this meeting escalated. Ben held her hand firmly as they walked along the corridor to the lounge room. Ben's family were here; the men avidly watched a game on television, and two women were chatting. Everyone's attention switched to Ben and Kennedy as they entered the room, and Kennedy relaxed when the greeting from his family members was warmer. Above the sound of the television, Kennedy heard chattering from another room, and then Mrs Foster called everyone for lunch.

When they entered the dining room, Kennedy felt Ben stiffen as he surveyed the people seated at the table. Ben swung to face his Mother.

"I told you at the last dinner that I would not attend if you invited the neighbours. I specifically requested you not to ask the Davidsons for this meal, and you agreed. Can I not trust you to keep your word?"

Mrs Foster looked at Ben as though he had lost his mind.

"When we have lunch together, I want all of my family here, and your invitation to the woman who saved that damned dog does not change my plans. Don't you think your new squeeze needs to meet your intended? Doesn't she deserve to know that you are committed to another woman?"

Ben looked furious, and as Kennedy watched him, she realised that this interference in his life might make their relationship difficult.

"Mrs Foster, when our family congregate, my Mother likes us to all attend. She wants my siblings and me to be happy with our lives. She doesn't wish us to be rich, famous, or great athletes. As a Mother, I would have assumed you wanted happiness for your children, but your interference in Ben's life causes him stress."

The woman Kennedy assumed was Mrs Davidson said,

"Ben changes women as fast as he changes socks. Don't think that you will become a fixture in Ben's life. When his damned dog is well, he will end your association, and he will return to Cherise."

Ben finally regained his ability to talk.

"Mother, you might consider these freeloaders as family, but they are not my family. Whether Kennedy and I continue our relationship will be up to us; if it doesn't work out, it will have nothing to do with Cherise. I asked you to promise you wouldn't invite the Davidsons, and you agreed. I can see that your word is worthless, and I will not believe a word you say in the future. You had a choice today: not invite the neighbours and I would attend, or invite them and deal with my absence. You've made your choice, and so have I. Enjoy your meal."

As Ben and Kennedy left the house, an argument broke out, but Kennedy didn't stop to listen. She wanted nothing more to do with the delusional woman. When Ben opened the car door for her, she reached up and kissed him. His arms came around her as he hugged her.

"I'm sorry about that. I thought my Mother would keep her word, but apparently, she'd rather have those guests than her son."

"It's her loss. But do you think you could go through a drive-through? I was looking forward to having a cooked lunch, but no matter how good the food was, I didn't want to endure the hostility."

After the aborted lunch, Ben drew back, and Kennedy wasn't confident whether the woman was right, and he would set her free when Duke was fit for service. Ben was on the day shift again, but it seemed he was not invested in their relationship, even though he wanted her to care for Duke. Kennedy continued her visits to feed Duke but struggled with Ben's withdrawal. When Ben arrived home, he went through the routines he was familiar with: securing his gun, removing his utility belt, and taking a shower. As he entered the patio where she sat with Duke, she said, "We need to talk." Ben watched Kennedy warily and nodded.

"Tell me what is going on in your head? You have withdrawn since that visit to your parents' house. Are you going to prove that Davidson woman right and ditch me now that Duke has almost recovered?"

"I'm struggling with deciding whether we should continue our relationship. The ridiculous assertion that I will marry Cherise seems to taint everything I do, and you are the best thing that has ever happened to me, but I don't want to let them taint what we have. I am worried that there will be pushback, and you will get caught in the crossfire."

"So, without consulting me, you will decide on our future? I must admit that when you told me about your mother's obsession with your marrying her best friend's daughter, I had reservations about getting involved with you. Ben, are you going to allow those women to ruin what we have? If you break off with me, does that mean you'll never have another relationship, out of fear of pushback? Will you marry that slag because it is the easiest thing to do? Please tell me you have more backbone than that."

"I will never marry Cherise, but I fear you will suffer more abuse and criticism."

"Ben, you are a policeman. I feel confident that you can protect me from the horrid women. It's not as though we mix in the same circles. Please do me a favour; don't believe anything your Mother or Cherise tell you about me in future. If I have anything to say, I will say it to your face. I don't think your Mother would become violent, but I do think she and Cherise may try to fill you with untruths to undermine our relationship."

Ben slid Kennedy from the couch to his lap, and Kennedy straddled his hips.

"Gosh, I've missed you, Ken."

Kennedy tilted Ben's head and kissed him. She had missed him, too, and she wouldn't let those delusional women ruin her relationship with Ben. As long as they kept their distance from her parents and the Davidsons, Kennedy felt confident they could build a strong relationship.

Chapter 10

The first phone call was hardly worrying, although Kennedy complained to Ben that people who dialled the wrong number should speak to the person who answered.

Some phone calls came to Ben's landline, while others went to her mobile when she was at home. The hang-ups were annoying, but when someone breathed heavily on the phone, Kennedy became anxious. What was happening? When she told Ben of her concerns, he passed them off as someone fooling around, but he didn't convince Kennedy. She tried blocking the calls, but they came from a burner phone, and she couldn't stop them.

Kennedy became frantic the morning she answered the phone, and a metallic voice spoke. Transfixed, she knew she should hang up, but the spine-tingling mechanical voice was cursing her and finally said, "I will get you, you fucking cunt; don't think I won't. When you least expect it, I will come after you."

Kennedy was shaking as the caller hung up, and even though she had to feed Duke at lunchtime, she still needed to report the call. Was this the result of being with Ben? She pushed that thought aside. The caller must be male because women called each other bitches, but not cunts. The sound of the word was crude and brutal.

Standing outside the police station, Kennedy began to second-guess herself. Was she overreacting? No, no, she wasn't. Ordinary people didn't make calls threatening others. Determined to report the call, Kennedy entered the building. The man behind the desk smiled and said, "What can I do for you?"

"I need to see Ben Foster."

"I'll see if he is available."

Ben looked harassed when he approached the reception desk, and the officer pointed to her. His eyes widened when he saw Kennedy, but there was no welcome in his face.

"Ken, I'm rushed off my feet. I don't have time for social calls, and it doesn't look good for you to be here. Is there a problem with Duke?"

"No, there's not a problem with Duke, but I need to..."

"Okay, I'm too busy now, but we'll talk when I get home."

Kennedy watched in amazement as Ben headed away from her. Now, what did she do? When Kennedy looked up, she realised the officer at the reception desk was watching her. Straightening her back, she approached the desk again.

"It seems my problem is not severe enough to concern Ben. Is there another person I can report a crime to?"

The officer nodded. "Give me a minute, and I'll get Constable Garrett here to talk to you."

A few minutes later, an officer walked towards her. He was tall and tanned, with smile lines around his eyes. Kennedy trusted him immediately, and when he suggested they head to his desk to discuss her problem, she followed him without hesitation.

"Now, tell me what your problem is."

Kennedy related the details about the first calls and ended with the last call. Officer Garret, whose name was Mike, jotted points on a pad and then said, "Can you think of anyone who might want to frighten you?"

" The language suggests the caller is a man because women call each other bitches, not the C word. One in a million women would use that word, so the chances are it's a man, and I have no idea why some bloke is threatening me."

Mike ran his hand through his hair and sighed.

"You know I'm going to tell you that there isn't much I can do, but there are some precautions you need to take. Call your mobile provider and report the calls in case they can block them from their end. Buy a personal security device that clips to your handbag or the tags on your jeans, and that makes a loud noise when you press the button. Check your security at home. Do you have deadlocks? Drive with the car doors locked and ask your neighbours to report any strange people loitering in the street. And let me know if the caller escalates. If I were you, I would stop answering phone calls where you don't recognise the number."

As Mike walked Kennedy out, she passed one of the women she had met at the bar.

"Hey, Kennedy, when will you join us at the pub?"

Kennedy smiled. "I didn't know whether you were serious when you invited me. When will you be there?"

Jill laughed. "Every Friday night."

"Okay, I'll join you next week."

Jill returned to her desk, and Mike grinned. "Your deeds and reputation are legendary around here."

Kennedy blushed. "I did what I thought was right, although punching someone in the face is something I've never done before."

Kennedy walked away from the station, pleased that Mike had taken her concerns seriously and with a shopping list of changes she needed to make. She would feed and medicate Duke; if Ben didn't call, she would head home. The way he brushed her off at the station still stung; Kennedy had never before been to his place of work, so why would he think her reason for being there was as frivolous as asking to join her for lunch? Sometimes, Kennedy wondered if she and Ben had a future, and that thought was not related to his family's resistance, but to the thoughtless way he occasionally acted towards her. His pulling back while he decided what was best for them was a prime example, and his reaction to her presence today was another red flag.

Kennedy checked her rear vision mirror as she drove, but no other cars were nearby, so she hoped the threat on the phone would not materialise. Ben rang to say he was running late but would pick up food on the way home. Kennedy was relieved not to have to worry about what to eat, as the to-do list consumed most of her day. A locksmith was coming to fit deadbolts and chains on the doors the next day. She had rung her mobile provider, and they agreed to block all calls from the burner phone. They could do this by refusing all calls not connected to a network and not fearing who was calling, which eased Kennedy's mind. A search online revealed numerous security devices, but Kennedy chose one small enough to hang unobtrusively on her belt. Her last job was to talk to Warren and Kay, who lived next door. She had only met her neighbours recently, but they had shared a barbecue and a potluck dinner, and Kennedy liked them.

When Ben arrived home, he placed the food containers in the warming drawer, chatted with Duke and then disappeared to remove his uniform and shower. The brief peck on her cheek when he entered the house lacked any warmth, and Kennedy was unsure whether Ben had endured a tough day or was rethinking their relationship again. While waiting for Ben, she walked out the back and sat beside Duke's bed. The thumping of his tail as he greeted her buoyed Kennedy's spirits.

"Why can't men be as easy to read as dogs? You are always happy to see me and never get cross. What's the issue with your master? Do you think we should show him your new tricks, or will he grumble about me teaching you skills that don't relate to your job?"

Noise in the kitchen suggested that Ben was showered and was dishing up dinner. The meal progressed quietly when Ben said, "I heard you agreed to go out with Jill, Kayla and crew. I thought I made my opinion of your calling at work clear. Nothing distracts from business more than civilians walking around unescorted. Please refrain from coming to the station again. Is that clear enough?"

Kennedy sat still, formulating a response that didn't escalate the tension. Eventually, she said, "I was not unescorted, as you assume. I reported a crime to Mike Garrett because he had time to listen to me. I saw the ladies as Mike escorted me out."

"What crime?"

As Kennedy described her terrifying phone call, Ben felt angry and mortified.

"Gosh, Ken, I'm an ass. It never occurred to me that you were there for official business."

"Well, that's something we agree on; you're an ass. We may have been together briefly, but I can't believe you think I would swan into the station in the hope of a quickie or morning tea. I don't believe I've ever behaved frivolously or given you a reason to doubt my sincerity."

"What did Mike suggest?"

Kennedy listed Mike's suggestions and identified the ones she had taken action on. Ben nodded. "I'm glad he was able to help, but the situation is troubling. Is there a man in your past who wants to hurt you?"

Kennedy shook her head. "No, no men wanting to cause trouble. You know, if this weren't a man harassing me, I might think your girlfriend was the perpetrator. Have you noticed that the phone calls started after our visit?"

"Yeah, but as you say, it is a man. I know Cherise and my Mother are delusional, but I don't believe they are criminals."

Pushing the troubling thoughts aside, Kennedy suggested they watch a movie. Before the credits rolled, Ben was asleep, so Kennedy lay him down, slid a pillow under his head and left the house quietly. As she drove home, Kennedy locked her doors, and her eyes constantly scanned her surroundings. When she pulled up under her carport, she realised the area was dark and decided to install action-activated lights under the carport and near the side door she used to enter.

Chapter 11

Kennedy rose early the following day to catch Warren and Kay at home before Warren left for work. When Kay answered the door, she smiled at Kennedy, although there was a hint of surprise in her eyes.

"Hi, Kay. Can I talk to you and Warren for a few minutes?"

Kay stepped away from the door, allowing Kennedy to enter.

Warren looked up as Kennedy entered.

"Good morning; what do we owe the pleasure?"

"Good morning. I have a problem, and I was hoping you could help. Recently, I've been receiving unusual phone calls. It started with hang-ups, then someone breathing heavily on the phone, and the last one was a mechanical voice promising to get me when I least expected it. I must confess that the last call was terrifying, so I reported it to the police. The officer and I think it is a man because he called me a fucking C word, and that's not something most women would use."

Kay nodded. "You're right. What can we do to help?"

"Mike, the policeman I reported to, suggested that you could keep an eye out for a strange man walking around. I don't want to put you in danger, so if you see someone, you could get a good description or call the cops."

Warren said, "What is this officer's name, and why didn't you tell the boyfriend all this? He's a cop too, isn't he?"

Kennedy flushed. "Ben and I had a miscommunication, so I reported it to Constable Mike Garrett."

Kay nodded. "I doubt that Warren will be helpful, considering he's out all day, but if I spot someone, I'll ring Constable Garrett, and we'll go from there."

Kennedy thanked her neighbours and returned home to wait for the locksmith.

Once the locksmith left, Kennedy drove to Ben's house. It surprised her that she hadn't heard from him this morning because she left last night without them having a chance to speak. Ben seemed a little peeved that Kennedy had reported the phone call to another officer, but after his tantrum at the station, she had no desire to discuss it with him. Kennedy remembered the concern she shared with Ben when the calls started, but he passed them off as pranks, so she felt better that Mike listened without patronising her.

Ben had left a cheery note on the bench, and Kennedy smiled at his sweet comments and apology for being a party pooper last night. After Kennedy fed and medicated Duke, she put him through his paces with the new tricks she had taught him and considered taking him for a walk. However, after her last attempt, she probably needed to muzzle him before taking him out in public again. Even though Kennedy was required to begin preparations for her class for the new year, she couldn't raise her enthusiasm for the task. Maybe she could take Duke for a drive; the ideal place would be to the vet. Kennedy rang Doctor Simmonds, and he said he would be delighted to see her and his patient, so Kennedy organised herself and, with Duke on a lead, she drove to the police veterinary office.

Duke was excited to see Doctor Simmonds, and the vet expressed his pleasure at how healthy Duke looked. After a quick check-up, Doctor Simmonds offered Kennedy a cup of tea, and she accepted. Duke lay at her feet, perfectly comfortable in her company, and the vet kept his concern about the bond that had grown between these two to himself. He worried that when Duke was ready for work, his confinement in the kennels might cause him distress because, although he would work with Ben, he would miss Kennedy.

Ben arrived on time and in a better frame of mind than yesterday. When he performed his nightly ritual, Kennedy was excited to show

Ben the tricks she had taught Duke. Ben raised his eyebrows as he watched his dog give Kennedy a high-five, and when she instructed Duke to play dead, he laughed as his dog rolled onto his back with his feet in the air.

"Gosh, Kennedy, you are turning my dog into a circus dog. God only knows if he can maintain his ferocious attitude once we get him back to work."

Kennedy laughed. "If his reaction to the bloke who wanted to pat him is any indication, that ferocious attitude will be present. Talking about ferocious, I want to take him for some walks, but considering his reaction the other day, he probably needs a muzzle. Have you got one I can use?"

Ben hunted around in a box and found a muzzle for Kennedy to use publicly.

Dinner that night was more relaxed, and as they ate, Ben raised the issue of the stalker.

"I have followed all of Mike's suggestions, and this morning, I spoke to my neighbours about a strange man in the area. I'm careful that nobody follows me when I leave home or leave here, so I guess that's the best I can do. He might lose interest if he can't reach me by phone. I can only hope. I should go."

"Can't you stay tonight? I promise not to fall asleep. Last night, I was angry, stressed and exhausted. Even if I sleep, I want to do it in my bed wrapped around you."

"So, you've stopped second-guessing our relationship?"

"Yeah, I want to protect you, but if the guy hassling you is because of me, I'd be a bastard to abandon you. Besides, I like you a lot, and so does my dog."

Kennedy laughed.

"God forbid if Duke hated me."

Kennedy groaned as Ben rose the following day. From the light filtering into the bedroom, it looked like it was just after dawn.

"What are you doing?"

"The commander asked me to stake out a suspect business, and as their main traffic period is after daybreak, I must leave now."

"Is someone accompanying you?"

"No, but it's only an observation. A task force will enter if the place warrants a closer inspection."

Ben sat on the edge of the bed and kissed Kennedy. She clung on for a minute, but knowing that he had to go, she eased herself away from him.

"Unless you want to upset your boss by not observing, you'd better leave before I pull you back into bed."

Ben grinned. "Hold that thought for tonight."

Chapter 12

With Christmas only a few days away, Kennedy was in a quandary. Duke still needed his medication and regular feeds, but all officers without children were on call on Christmas Eve and Christmas Day. That meant Ben would be gone for more than twenty-four hours, so the feeding and medication fell to Kennedy. Kennedy and Claire were travelling to the retirement village where her parents resided for the day, leaving Duke unattended. Kennedy broached the subject when Ben came home.

"Can Duke spend a day or two in the kennels? I would take him with me, but I'm not sure what the dog policy at the village is, and if he dislikes some of the residents, it would be most uncomfortable."

"Yeah, sure, I'll contact the kennel master and explain the situation. When are you leaving?"

"Claire is going to drive, and we'll be away for three or four days. If you permit me, I can collect Duke when I return if you're still tied up."

Ben snagged Kennedy around the waist and pulled her toward himself.

"I know I won't be home, but I like knowing you're in my house."

Kennedy turned in Ben's arms and grabbed his biceps to anchor herself as she kissed him. As Ben took control of the kiss, Kennedy knew he would await her when she returned. Despite her doubts, there was no confusion about his desire for her when he steered her to the bedroom.

Claire and Kennedy arrived at the retirement village late in the afternoon. Tomorrow was Christmas Eve, and their parents had organised a lights tour for themselves and their daughters. At this time of year, Kennedy always felt sad, knowing Nick was far away in some foreign country. Her family made a care package to send each Christmas, but as far as she was concerned, it was time for him to come home.

Christmas day went off without a hitch, and rather than drive home on Boxing Day, Claire and Kennedy decided to stay. Kennedy suspected Ben would be out on the roads, booking motorists and patrolling hotspots, so returning at the moment wasn't a priority. Two days later, they headed home, leaving their parents to prepare for the New Year's Eve party. Even though Kennedy enjoyed a party, the thought of watching senior citizens cavorting together was not high on her list. The sisters shared the driving and occasionally stopped at a diner or a coffee shop, but once they reached the outskirts of town, Kennedy was looking forward to sleeping in her bed. Her text messages to Ben had gone unanswered, and she assumed he was still working.

She sighed when Claire turned the corner of her street, but that relief disappeared as they pulled into her driveway. The girls sat transfixed until Kennedy let out a wail. Scrambling from Claire's car, Kennedy raced to stand next to her vehicle. An empty egg carton lay on the ground beside the car; egg yolks and whites covered the vehicle. Every inch of the car was covered, and the hardened substance suggested that someone had egged it a day or two before their arrival. Never in her wildest dreams did Kennedy think she would return to her ruined car. While she had asked her neighbours to look out for strangers, she knew they had also gone away for Christmas, so the perpetrator had free rein to ruin her vehicle. Claire was the first one to find her voice.

"What the fuck?"

Tears streaked Kennedy's cheeks as she gazed at her vehicle.

"Well, Merry Christmas to me."

Kennedy regretted not telling Claire about the stalker, but she updated her, then dialled the police station and asked for Mike Garrett.

"Merry Christmas, Kennedy. What can I do for you?"

Kennedy was weeping so hard that Mike couldn't make sense of her complaint, so Claire took the phone from her sister. Claire explained to Mike why Kennedy had rung him. He swore and told them not to enter the house until he had checked that it was safe.

When Mike finished taking photos of the car and gave Kennedy a crime number, he suggested she organise a tow truck for her vehicle, as the egg had ruined the paint and it would need to be spray-painted. While she rang a tow truck, Mike entered Kennedy's house to check that all was well. As he moved from room to room, he chaffed at his inability to resolve the issue of Kennedy's stalker. Who was it who wanted to cause her grief? What had Kennedy done to evoke this level of hostility?

Outside the house, Mike waited as the tow truck hitched up Kennedy's car. He could do little without evidence or an eyewitness, but he suggested that Kennedy spend the night at her sister's house. Against his better judgment, Mike approached Kennedy and said, "Where is Ben tonight? He's not on duty."

Kennedy shrugged. "I told him we would be home this afternoon, but he hasn't replied. Why?'

Mike stepped closer. "Because you look like you need a hug, and while I don't want to step on any toes, I'm willing to be a substitute."

Kennedy stepped towards Mike, and he wrapped his arms around her. As Mike embraced Kennedy, she felt safe and secure, feelings that had fled when she first viewed her car. After a few moments, she sighed and stepped back.

"Thank you, that gives a whole new meaning to community policing."

Mike waited until the girls pulled away before driving his squad car back to the station.

Mike slid the newest piece of evidence into the McCann folder at the station. He strolled through the bullpen and towards the

Commander's office. Although the man was old-school and often abrupt, Mike wanted to inform him about the latest incident involving Kennedy and ask for his suggestions.

"Could someone have a beef against the woman for finding Foster's dog?"

When the commander posed the question, it was a view Mike hadn't investigated.

"When he's next on duty, question Foster. It seems to me that it is too much of a coincidence that the harassment of the McCann girl happened after she found the dog. His family were not supportive when he changed to the dog squad, so that might be an angle worth investigating."

Mike thanked his boss, and with his new perspective on Kennedy's harassment, he felt he at least had an avenue of enquiry.

Chapter 13

Without contact from Ben, Kennedy was unsure whether or not he expected her at his house that day. Shrugging, she decided to visit Ben, and if he didn't need her help, she would spend the day on the phone with her insurance company. Even though Ben's house was only a few blocks away, she would need to hire a car until the repairers fixed her car's bodywork, because walking that short distance at night was not a safe option given the level of harassment she was receiving.

Ben had parked his car in the driveway, but Kennedy rang the bell instead of using her key. When he answered her door, his dishevelled appearance suggested he had not long risen. She smiled at his appearance and moved towards him to kiss him, but Ben moved away. Confused and hurt, Kennedy was unsure what to do.

"Um, we didn't make any plans for Duke's care after the Christmas break, and I thought I would check with you to see what we are doing."

Ben sighed and stepped back, allowing Kennedy to enter.

"Give me a minute to clean up, and we can talk."

When Ben walked away, Kennedy started the coffee maker and walked to the sunroom to see if Duke was there. His bed was empty, and Kennedy wondered why, if he had been off for two days, he hadn't collected his dog. Ten minutes later, Ben appeared, his hair still wet from his shower but still unshaven.

"I didn't expect you today."

Kennedy cocked her head to the side and said, "Why not?"

"Well, you're not answering my phone. Ghosting me for the last week doesn't encourage me to expect you to carry out your commitment."

" Ghosting you?"

Kennedy stared at Ben and pulled her phone from her pocket. Holding the screen face towards him, she showed him the text messages she had sent and played the voice messages she had left.

"I'm not sure what the problem is with your phone, but I have rung and texted you numerous times since I left. Is Duke still at the kennels? If you've been off, why haven't you collected him?"

Ben sighed. "I need coffee before we discuss this problem."

Kennedy followed Ben into the kitchen and propped herself at the bench. Neither said anything until Ben placed a mug for each of them on the bench top and took a seat. He handed Kennedy his phone, and as she scrolled through it, she could see the calls and texts he had made to her.

"What the hell?"

Kennedy punched Ben's number into her phone and put her device on speaker. Ben's phone on the bench remained silent, but Kennedy's phone gave her the message that the device was off or out of range.

"What the hell indeed?"

"Now you know I'm not ghosting you; where is Duke?"

"I texted you and asked if you could collect him, but since you didn't arrive here with my dog and didn't answer me, I was going to get him today. Sorting out the phone could take ages, so let's get Duke and work out the problem with my phone later."

"I'll move my car. We will need to use your ute because I have hired a car. When Claire and I returned from our trip, somebody had egged my car. May I add that it wasn't just one or two eggs, but an entire carton, and it appeared to have been done shortly after we left? The egg has destroyed the paintwork. It needs to be re-sprayed, so I hope the insurance company pay for the repairs."

"Why would somebody vandalise your car? Did you report the damage to the patrol?"

"Yes, I reported the damage, and the answer to the first question is that whoever the maniac is sending me messages has escalated now that they can't reach me on the phone."

"I'm sorry, I assumed the calls you received were nuisance calls; it seems someone has a vendetta against you. Let's get Duke, and we can sort out the rest later."

"Now that you're not angry with me, do I get a welcome home kiss?"

Ben smiled and pulled Kennedy against him. He removed the hair tie from around her ponytail and fisted her hair. Ben placed kisses all over Kennedy's face, and she was laughing and pleading by the time he reached her lips. Kennedy decided the kiss was worth waiting for, and she responded with equal enthusiasm. She sighed when Ben moved back.

"I missed you, even though my holiday was enjoyable. What did you do?"

"Let's go, and we can talk as I drive."

The drive to the kennels gave them time to catch up. Kennedy felt sad for Ben, and even though he couldn't spend Christmas day with his family, his mother insisted on inviting her neighbours to the meal that Ben attended three days later. She knew the kind of pressure the women would place on Ben, and she sympathised with him. Even if Ben loved the neighbours—which he didn't—never having a family meal without them would be annoying. The conversation ended when they reached the kennels, but Kennedy intended to suggest his family when they had time to talk further.

When the attendant went to collect Duke, Kennedy and Ben waited in the reception area. Minutes later, they could hear scrabbling paw sounds, and as the door burst open, Duke lunged at Ben. After his exuberant welcome to Ben, Duke disengaged and gave Kennedy the same enthusiastic greeting. The attendant laughed.

"I should feel offended that your dog is so excited to see you both, but I know dogs want to be where their people are. Will we see him back here?"

"I'm not sure what will happen. Duke must pass a fitness test before he can resume his duties, but we move closer to total health every day. He might need a refresher course, so it would be easier if he were here, but I know this is not his favourite place. When we drive in here, he looks like I'm taking him to jail; he's a homebody even though he's trained to apprehend villains."

After the excitement of greeting Kennedy and Ben, Duke lay quietly in his crate in the back of the vehicle. Ben and Kennedy chatted until they reached home.

"Before you attempt to rectify whatever is wrong with your phone, I have a question or two."

"Let me get Duke a treat and a drink for us. Come and sit outside, and you can ask your questions."

Sitting in the easy chairs under the patio, Ben said, "Ask away."

"You had a meal with your family while I was away. Had you tried contacting me before lunch?"

"No, I was on duty, and we were running breathalizers and speed checks, so that meal was my first downtime. After the stress of the meal, I thought I would call you; then, I had something good to look forward to. Why?"

"One more question first. You placed your wallet and phone on the bench beside the kitchen door the last time we visited. Is that where you left it?"

Ben groaned. "Yes."

"You know what I'm going to say, don't you?"

"Yeah, I do. It looks like I spend hours talking to my telco to see how someone changed my settings."

"If you invite me to stay, I'll start dinner."

Kennedy could hear Ben's voice rise as he talked to the people responsible for their inability to communicate. Considering that most devices and settings required a passcode, Kennedy wondered whether Ben's password was strong enough to deter a determined person, or if he used something easy, like his birthdate. An hour after he started his call, Ben had convinced the telco that the changes to his settings were unauthorised, and they reversed the block put in place to prevent him from making or receiving calls from Kennedy.

Chapter 14

When Kennedy woke the following day, she discovered Ben had already left for work. After feeding Duke, she had to contact her insurer and check in on Mike to see if he had found anything to help identify the culprit. The harassment and vandalism coincided with her meeting with Ben's family. Was one of them responsible? Did they think Ben would end the relationship and return to Cherise if they made things complicated between them? When Ben shared his family history, Kennedy remembered that she had wondered if associating with Ben was worth the trouble. Kennedy pushed the thoughts aside; the culprit must be a deranged person who had fixated on her.

Aside from a quick trip back to Ben's house to feed Duke his lunch, Kennedy had spent most of the day rearranging boxes and furniture and chasing the insurance company to come and assess her car. Ben would finish work soon, and she could ring and tell him she wasn't coming over, or she could pick up some food and spend a quiet night with him. Even though she was tired, Kennedy missed Ben when they were apart, so deciding to have dinner with him was easy. Having been alone for most of the day, Duke was pleased to see her, and Kennedy spent time fussing over him and chatting to him. The sound of the key in the lock surprised Kennedy because she hadn't expected Ben home so early, but Duke's response to the noise told her it was not Ben at the door. As the door moved open, Duke lunged at the flyscreen door and growled low in his throat.

Kennedy was as stunned as Duke was agitated when Cherise walked into the house carrying grocery bags, although she hesitated when she heard Duke's growls. Kennedy spent a moment calming Duke and then stalked into the kitchen.

"What are you doing here, and how did you get the key?"

Cherise glared at Kennedy.

"Mother Foster gave me the key because we decided Ben needed a home-cooked meal when he returned from work."

"So, without consulting Ben about his plans, you and his Mother decided to invade his house?"

Cherise laughed. "What makes you think Ben doesn't know? You've done your job of babysitting the dog, so get lost. When you can't use the dog as an excuse to see Ben, he'll tell you to take a hike. You didn't think he was into you, did you? "

"You and Mrs Foster must be delusional. I haven't known Ben long, but he is firm on not wanting anything to do with you."

"Fuck off, cunt. You are the delusional one."

After Kennedy collected her things, she gave Duke a treat and calmed him before she walked out the door. She tried to call Ben, but he was unavailable, so she headed home, confident they could sort out the problem the next day.

Ben frowned at the strange car parked in his driveway and wondered if Kennedy had changed her rental vehicle. When he opened the door, he heard Duke growling, and the voice that ordered "the bloody mongrel" to shut up was not Kennedy's.

"What the hell are you doing here? How did you get in?"

"I'm here to cook you a nice meal instead of eating takeaway all the time; you know it's not good for you. Regarding the other question, your babysitter let me in; she seemed relieved she wouldn't have to stay for the meal, even though I had offered to stay. She was excited to ditch the dog because she planned a night out."

Ben could make no sense of what Cherise said. Would Kennedy let a woman he hated into his home to make him a meal? Did Kennedy want some entertainment that didn't include Duke and him?

"Have your shower, and the meal will be ready."

"I'll ring Kennedy before I eat."

"She won't thank you for interrupting her night out. Text her after we eat."

The text message chimed as Kennedy washed the dishes from her solitary meal. It didn't sound like Ben was angry at Cherise's appearance, and she shook her head. Acknowledging Ben's text, Kennedy walked to the next-door neighbours to see if they wanted to chat. She realised she hadn't spoken to them since the vandalism of her car, and Kennedy needed some time out from the confusing relationship she had with Ben. Perhaps Kay or Warren could offer her some insight into the mood swings and trust issues that have plagued their relationship. Warren recommended that Kennedy put the rental in the garage because if the car were accessible, the stalker might deface it. His other suggestion was to have her roll-down automated so she didn't have to leave the car to open the door. Kennedy decided to follow Warren's suggestions and vowed to move the boxes out of the garage, making room for the vehicle. She gave her neighbours a front-door key and promised to leave a garage-door remote with the couple the next day or two.

Kennedy walked to her rental car to feed Duke at Ben's the following day. She screwed up her face as she tried to decipher the red scrawls on the road in front of her house; walking to the curb, Kennedy could read the writing. She sighed. Did writing on the street in red paint count as vandalism? Kennedy dialled Mike's number, hoping he was on duty. It took an hour for Mike's squad car to arrive, and his curse reflected how she felt. Once he had collected the photo evidence, Mike suggested she come into the station to give a brief statement.

"Can I do that later? I have to feed Duke, and Ben and I are meeting for lunch, so I'll tell him what happened."

"Why don't you come and make the statement before you talk to Ben? I advised the boss of how your case had escalated, and he made a suggestion that I'd like to discuss with you."

When Kennedy entered the station, she encountered the same officer at the front desk. After greeting her, he contacted Mike, who came to meet her. Today, Mike didn't stop when they reached his desk, but continued until they arrived at a small interrogation room. Kennedy raised her eyebrow as Mike ushered into the room, and he answered her silent query.

"I want to talk to you privately because what I have to suggest will be uncomfortable to hear. The boss pointed out that the calls and general harassment started after you found Duke. Is that right?"

"No, they started after I met Ben's family. Do you remember I said that because of the language used, I thought the person harassing me was a man?"

"Yes, have you reconsidered your thoughts?"

"Yes. Last night, Ben's intended let herself into the house before he arrived home. We argued, and you'll never guess what she called me?"

Mike nodded. "Ah, you don't need to spell it out; it appears she is one of the rare women you named when this first happened."

" I spent all night reviewing the things that have happened since I met the Foster and Davidson families, and I believe it is either Ben's Mother or the Davidson woman loading the gun, and Cherise is firing the bullets."

"The boss wanted me to approach Ben about that thought, but it would be hard to prosecute that argument without further evidence."

"So what do we do?"

Mike glanced at his watch. "Let's meet Ben for lunch, and I'll raise the question of his family and neighbours' involvement. If he balks, you can mention the argument with the woman and the language she used. We can't prosecute either woman without evidence, but it might stop if Ben accuses them and tells them what they are doing is a criminal offence."

"I know Ben will be angry if we suggest his Mother or the Davidsons are involved, so I am glad you are coming with me. Hopefully, if they are involved and listen to him, the pestering will stop."

Chapter 15

Ben checked his watch; Kennedy was running late, as usual. When a person walked up behind him, he swung around to greet Kennedy when he realised his companion was Cherise. His scowl at her made his anger at her arrival apparent, but she ignored his glare and sat opposite Ben.

"What the hell are you doing here?"

"Don't be like that. I came to tell you not to waste your time waiting for Kennedy. I just saw her and a handsome police officer get out of a car, and when they met up on the footpath, he hugged her and gave her a kiss that was not a brotherly peck, if you get my meaning."

Ben looked Cherise in the eye, trying to decide whether her account of Kennedy with another officer was valid or a deceptive statement. He shook his head when she took his hands in hers and held them. Cherise had always been a convincing liar; was Kennedy involved with someone else, or was Cherise lying? Damn, how had this got so complicated? Kennedy finding Duke should have been the end of their involvement, but he let Kennedy into his life and his bed, and now he couldn't decide if she was cheating on him. When Ben remembered Kennedy's reporting to Mike, he concluded that she had tricked him, and even if she was genuine at the beginning, she had changed her allegiance to Mike.

Mike found a parking spot close to the open-air eating space where Ben had suggested they meet, and they walked along the footpath towards the meeting place. Kennedy stopped and looked at Mike.

"Are we doing the right thing?"

"We must do something, or the culprit's actions might injure you. What started as phone calls escalated the moment you cut off the connection. It might be that the escalation would not have happened had they still made contact on the phone, but in my experience, the harassment usually intensifies."

Kennedy nodded and resumed walking. When she and Mike arrived at the entrance, she scanned the area for Ben. Her gaze rested on her boyfriend sitting opposite the woman he said he hated. They held hands across the table as they gazed into each other's faces. Kennedy stepped back, and Mike sighed.

"The man is an idiot. Your meeting is a bust, and so is my opportunity to broach the subject of his involvement. I'm sorry the man is so unpredictable, although if you had asked me months ago, I would have said he was a steady bloke and a good officer. What do you want to do now?"

Kennedy still felt dazed at what she had witnessed, and she thanked Mike for his assistance as she walked away. She intended to go through a drive-through, feed Duke and call a contractor to automate her garage door. Kennedy would spend the remainder of the day stacking the packing boxes away to make room for the rental vehicle tonight. It seemed her relationship with Ben had ended, and she cursed herself for not listening to her instincts when he first told her about his family history.

Later in the day, Ben's name showed on her phone's display, and Kennedy answered the phone with trepidation. Would Ben ask why she hadn't met him at lunchtime, or would he come clean about his involvement with Cherise? Neither of her predictions came true; Ben said he no longer needed her help and wanted her to leave the key at the house the next day. After he made his statement, he gave Kennedy no opportunity to reply before he ended the call.

The next day, after Kennedy left the house key on the kitchen bench, she searched for Duke. His bed and the dog bowls were missing, and the medicine she kept in the pantry was gone as well. Due to the lack of dog-related equipment, Ben had once again abandoned his dog at the police kennels. Kennedy felt sad that she couldn't say goodbye to Duke and realised that Mrs Davidson had been right when she told Kennedy that Ben would break off their friendship when Duke was well. She removed her toiletries from the bathroom and collected the clothes she had left behind the last time she was here. Ensuring that there was no trace of her left behind, Kennedy closed the door for the last time.

Kennedy spent the next few days preparing for the upcoming school year, which was approaching fast. At night, she binge-watched a new series and spent the evening trying to clear her mind of thoughts of Ben and catch up on sleep. Kennedy regretted becoming involved with Ben, and her heart broke at his callous treatment of her. Who asked their girlfriend to meet them and then invited another woman to join them? She was sure her initial assessment of him was correct, so what went wrong? It seemed that since Ben ended their relationship, the harassment stopped, which convinced her that her conclusion that Cherise and one of the Mothers were responsible for causing her anxiety and financial hardship was correct. Kennedy didn't believe in coincidences; the cessation of the harassment, coming simultaneously with their breakup, spoke volumes. It seemed there was no point continuing to hassle her now that Ben was firmly in the grip of his controlling family.

Kennedy sighed as she saw the last of her students off. The first day back was always stressful as students adjusted to a new room and teacher. The hierarchy often split the previous class, so the students had a new cohort to become acquainted with. Kennedy packed her supplies away and headed for the staffroom, where they held the first meeting of the year. There was no heavy agenda today; the meeting was to ensure that new staff had no difficulties and that any problems arising from the class split could be resolved.

Claire expected Kennedy for dinner tonight, and the thought of Claire's home-style cooking appealed greatly. When she and Ben were together, Kennedy often cooked, but the idea of cooking for herself was too much of a bother. Since Kennedy and Ben split up, she had taken to buying take-out or cooking microwave dinners. When she pulled into Claire's driveway, Kennedy felt her spirits rise. Tonight would involve comfort food, wine, and decadent dessert. If this were not a school night, Kennedy might be tempted to stay over with her sister, but the thought of rushing in the morning didn't appeal.

Their night ended early because both sisters had jobs to attend tomorrow, so as Kennedy drove through the quiet streets of her suburb, she felt relaxed and content. The bad things that happened while she was with Ben had stopped, and even though she regretted their relationship ending, she was glad that she was no longer the focus of a mad person. Even though things seemed quiet, Kennedy used the remote to open her garage door and parked the rental in the garage. The thought of another enormous insurance bill for damage to her current vehicle made her even more cautious. She hoped the panel beaters would soon finish her car so she could return the rental. However, for now, it was her mode of transport, and she needed to protect it in case her tormentors had more vandalism in mind.

Before turning in, Kennedy flicked on the television to keep her company. When she heard the dramatic music signalling breaking news, she wandered back into the lounge room to see what had happened. Her body froze when the presenter started his report, citing the altercation between the police and a criminal. As the man fled, Constable Ben Foster released his dog to apprehend the man, and the dog sustained stab injuries. The reporter continued with his account of the incident, reminding viewers that the handler lost this dog for months at the end of the year.

Tears ran down Kennedy's face as she grieved for Duke. The reporter continued with his spiel by saying the story had a happy ending as the dog had sustained serious but not life-threatening injuries. While the reporter wanted to interview Ben, he settled for an apprehension team member. The officer laughed as he related the most fantastic thing about the incident.

"When Constable Foster sent his dog to apprehend the suspect, the man produced a pocket knife and stabbed the dog as it hung off his arm. Duke dropped to the ground, but as he prepared to attack again, the guy started to lunge for him. Ben yelled, "Play dead." And the dog dropped like a stone and allowed me to taser the suspect."

Kennedy slumped into the chair as the danger both Ben and Duke face hit her. Despite her falling out with Ben, Kennedy wanted to see Duke. She rang the veterinary clinic, but a recording answered. With her car keys clenched in her fist, Kennedy debated for a few minutes, grabbed her bag, and headed to the car. When she arrived at Ben's house, all the lights were on. It looked as though Ben had every light in the place turned on. Bracing herself, Kennedy walked to the front door and banged. When Cherise answered the door, Kennedy snarled at her.

"I want to see Duke,"

"Tough luck for you. Ben doesn't want to see you."

Kennedy sized up the other woman and said, "I don't give a toss about Ben; you can have him. I want to see Duke."

As the woman moved to close the door, Kennedy shoved hard, and the door flew open, and the woman landed on the floor. The noise attracted the interest of the police officers and family who filled the lounge room, and Kennedy waded through the crowd until she reached Ben.

"Where is he?"

"On his bed, but wait; I have to say thank you. He would be dead if you hadn't taught him that stupid trick. When the guy produced the knife, I knew that shouting for release wouldn't have an instant response, and if he was to survive, I needed an instant response. Your trick saved his life."

Kennedy nodded. "Please, can I see him?"

Although Doctor Simmonds had sedated him, Duke wagged his tail slowly as Kennedy approached. Crouching on the ground beside his bed, she patted his neck and ran her hand through his long coat. With her face pressed against his neck, she breathed in his doggy smell, although the odours of antiseptic and bandages seeped through. Kennedy remained with Duke as the visitors inside chatted.

"You did well, Kennedy. You seem to be his guardian angel."

Kennedy looked up to see Doctor Simmonds standing near her. She rose to speak to him, but tears poured from her eyes. The vet pulled her into a hug and held on while Kennedy cried. When the tears dried, she said, "I heard it on the news, and I couldn't breathe until the reporter said he was alive. I couldn't believe I saved him once, only to have him die apprehending a criminal."

"Sweetheart, you have saved him twice, and I, for one, am grateful."

Kennedy gave Duke another pat and said, "I had better leave because half of the people in the loungeroom hate me."

"And the other half love what you did to save Duke last time and will rib Ben forever for letting you teach his service dog tricks."

The vet escorted Kennedy as she wended her way through the crowd. Half the group glared at her, but the others high-fived and patted her. The kind man walked her to her car and watched as she drove away. Returning to the house, he suggested that the officers who had come to support Ben go home, but before he left, he said, "She saved your damn dog twice, and you didn't think to notify her that although he was injured, he would live?"

Before Ben could answer the vet's comment, Cherise barged in and said.

"Why should Ben notify that skank? Just because she was in the right place the first time doesn't make her a hero. What happened here has nothing to do with her."

Doctor Simmonds stared at the belligerent woman, raising an eyebrow.

"Ben should have contacted her as a matter of courtesy, a word I'm sure you'll have to Google to discover the meaning. What a sad individual you are if you have to belittle Kennedy after all she has done for Ben and Duke. From the little I've seen of you, she is worth ten times more than you."

Doctor Simmonds turned to Ben, saying, "Keep him quiet and give him the antibiotics. He should be up and about in a day or two, but he won't be fit for duty for about a month."

Ben watched as the vet walked away, and as he sighed, he realised his Father stood close.

"Why didn't you ring her?"

Ben shrugged. "I didn't think she would want to talk to me."

His Father shook his head. "She doesn't want to talk to you, but she loves that dog. All the officers here hold her in high regard; they wouldn't have given her high fives and pats on the back if they didn't. After all she did for you and Duke, I fail to understand your treatment of her. I realise you are no longer together, and I don't know what happened, but if I had to guess, I'd say Cherise had something to do with your break-up. Sometimes, when I look at you, I wonder where I failed."

Ben glared at his Father. It had been a stressful day, and he wanted his family to go home and leave him alone. The thing his Father said about suspecting Cherise had a hand in his break-up with Kennedy resonated. Did Cherise lie about seeing Kennedy with another man? Kennedy hadn't offered any defence when he rang to tell her that he was finishing the agreement about caring for Duke and for her to leave her key, but Ben realised he hadn't allowed her to question him or defend herself. How could his life become so complicated? When Duke disappeared, it shattered him because he knew his time in the dog squad was on hold until they trained another dog. Training a dog was expensive and time-consuming, and even if the kennel masters found a suitable dog, it could take up to twelve months before the dog was ready for duty. Duke's rescue by Kennedy was a dream he never thought would come true, and in rescuing his partner, he also met a fantastic woman. Kennedy was kind, compassionate, cheeky and a cheater? It didn't gel, and for the first time, he wondered if his Father was correct in assuming Cherise had something to do with his estrangement from Kennedy.

Chapter 16

The sound of shattering glass woke Kennedy. Sleep left her disoriented and muddled, and it took a few moments to react to the continued smashing sounds. As she left her bed to investigate, Kenny realised that glass shards covered her bed and the floor surrounding it. In the dim light, Kennedy stumbled to the door, attempting to make sense of the continued crashing and the tinkle of glass in her house. Hunting for a light switch, she hesitated before illuminating the room. Would the attacker stop with the place lit, or would the brazen attacker continue regardless? Kennedy felt blood trickle down her face, her feet ached, and thankfully, the sounds had stopped. She hunted for her phone, cursing, when she realised it was on the charger in her room. Picking her way amongst the shards of glass, Kennedy reached her bedroom. She dialled triple zero with shaking hands and asked for police and an ambulance.

What should she do while she waited for the emergency vehicles to arrive? Moving around was dangerous, as the entire house seemed to be covered in glass. Not a single chair had escaped the shower of glass, so sitting was out of the question. The sound of a vehicle pulling up outside made Kennedy anxious; was this the police or the attacker returning? When she heard loud banging on the front door, she cautiously approached.

"Police, Ms McCann, open the door."

With relief, Kennedy opened the door. The sight of the two police officers and the approaching ambulance shattered her reserve, and she sobbed as she tried to tell the officers what transpired. The paramedics set Kennedy on their stretcher and checked the cuts on her feet and the gashes on her face. Glass shards had sliced Kennedy's cheek open and had damaged her feet so badly that walking was a challenge. Pieces of glass embedded in the soles of her feet and sprinkled among her hair and clothes convinced the medics that they should treat Kennedy at the hospital. Another car pulled up before the ambulance officers loaded her in. With relief, Kennedy recognised the man; Mike Garrett felt like her saviour. Whenever something bad happened, he rode to her rescue. He approached her, a grimace on his face as he surveyed the destruction in her house.

"Damnation, Kennedy, I thought these senseless acts of violence had stopped now that you and Ben aren't together, but I guess I was wrong."

Kennedy nodded. "I rejoiced that this madness had stopped, but my celebration was premature."

Sobs interrupted Kennedy's conversation with Mike. "What did I do to deserve this treatment? How can someone I hardly know hate me this much?"

Kennedy's head shot up when she heard one of the officers say, "You can't go in there; it's a crime scene."

A male voice said, "Please, tell me that Kennedy is alright."

Kennedy asked the officer to let Warren stand on the steps to talk to her, and when Warren saw him, he gave her a grim smile. Her response came out as a wail, but Kennedy could not remove the despair from her voice.

"Look at my house. Why would someone do this?"

"I'll get Kay, and we'll follow you to the hospital. You can spend the night with us and worry about this mess tomorrow."

Mike intervened. "You're the Warren that Kennedy was telling me about?"

When Warren nodded, Mike said, "You are kind to offer a refuge for Kennedy tonight, but that will be the first place the lunatic looks, and it could place you in danger. Kennedy can stay with me. I live alone, but I will ring my Mother to come and stay, so you have another woman to tend your cuts and provide a shoulder to cry on. Ken, I'll collect you from the hospital shortly, but we must call someone to secure your house."

"Garrett, we need Ms McCann to make a statement."

Mike nodded. "I'll personally deliver her to the station in the morning."

When Mike arrived at the hospital, he shook his head when he saw the stitches on Kennedy's face and the bandages covering her feet. Her hair appeared free of glass, and she wore a pair of scrubs instead of the pyjamas covered in blood and glass. Kennedy manoeuvred herself into the waiting wheelchair loaded with antibiotic creams and extra dressings; they made their way to the entrance. Mike had parked his vehicle in front of the doors, and Kennedy wheeled towards the side of the car. As she wriggled to raise herself from the chair, Mike said, "Oh, no, you don't. Give me your things, and I'll lift you into the car. Didn't the doctor say to keep off your feet?"

Kennedy felt awkward when Mike carried her from the car to his front door, where a woman whom Kennedy assumed was Mike's Mother greeted them. Before he made introductions, Mike carried Kennedy into a cosy bedroom and placed her on the bed. As he lowered her, he groaned and, looking at his Mother, he said, "Don't go feeding her too much, or I'll need a crane truck to move her."

Kennedy squealed. "If I didn't like you so much, I might get up the energy to be angry. Can I go to sleep now and worry about everything else tomorrow?"

"Yes, I bet the painkillers are kicking in. Before you sleep, please meet my mum, Sandra. I probably won't be here when you rise, but I'll return around ten to take you to the station to make a statement."

Kennedy smiled at Sandra, and then Mother and Son left her room. She thought making herself comfortable might be hard, considering the lacerations on her body, but when her head hit the pillow, she went out like a light. Sandra sat at the kitchen table as Mike poured cups of tea.

"Tell me about your friend. I assume she's not your girlfriend, or I wouldn't be here."

Mike sat at the table and sighed.

"No, she's not my girlfriend, but I hate what is happening to her and wanted to keep her safe tonight. It's a long and complicated story that started when Kennedy found one of the dogs from the dog squad that had gone missing a month or two before."

"I remember reading about that, but how did it deteriorate to someone causing Kennedy harm?"

As the details unfolded, Sandra grew increasingly concerned for the girl, who seemed to be the target of a madman. Mike continued. "The problem becomes tricky because Kennedy is confident that her tormentor is Ben Foster's ex-girlfriend. From the instances and the timing of the attacks, the commander and I think Kennedy is correct, but we have no concrete evidence. Accusing the woman of a crime is tricky, but after today, I'll check with the commander and talk to Ben. I don't believe he knows about these attacks, but as a cop, he must have a gut feeling that it's too much of a coincidence the attacks started when Kennedy met his family."

"That poor girl. She did a good turn finding the dog and nursed him for months, only to have her life turned upside down. I'll get her breakfast in the morning and clean her up before you collect her. I might consider hiring a wheelchair. The design of your house is not wheelchair friendly, but keeping her off her feet is a priority."

Chapter 17

Ben glared at Mike. "What the hell are you talking about? Why would my family or neighbours be involved in Kennedy's harassment? Considering her behaviour with me, she probably has an angry ex or a spurned lover in her past who is getting revenge."

Mike shook his head. "I'll ignore that ignorant, uninformed comment and return to the most pressing issue. As a copper, you're supposed to be able to look at the circumstantial evidence and try to come to a conclusion. Don't you think the phone calls starting right after Kennedy met your family and neighbours are too much of a coincidence? And if my girlfriend were receiving hang-ups and heavy breathing on the phone, I would move heaven and earth to find the culprit. But not you; you told her it was wrong numbers first, and then teenagers next. Did you know who made the calls and did not want Kennedy to make a fuss?"

Ben shot out of his seat. "Of course, I didn't know. How could I? The hang-ups didn't concern me, but when she started receiving heavy-breathing calls, I asked Jaffa to trace them; however, they came from a burner phone. The day she came to report the call, the boss was on my tail, wanting the last month's car theft figures, and I blew her off. I thought she had come to have lunch with me, and I didn't have time for that."

"Because, of course, she is so entitled that she would come to the station and expect you to drop everything and take her out. Has she ever given you the impression that she is flighty and entitled? No, she hasn't. Are you not concerned that someone severely egged her car while she was away for Christmas, ruining the duco? The re-spray job will cost thousands."

Ben ran his hands through his hair in frustration.

"She told me about that, but I was trying to sort out what happened to our phones, and I guess it slipped from my mind. I didn't see the car; Kennedy had hired a rental the day after the vandalism. I feel sorry for Kennedy, but I don't see what this has to do with me."

Mike ignored Ben's comment."The latest episode was last night when someone hurled bricks through each of the plate-glass windows at the front of Kennedy's house, showering her with glass. She is currently in a safe place, but because the glass shards cut her feet and the laceration on her face required stitches, she is lying low. My concern is whether this will be the last of the harassment she has to endure or if there will be more to come. If this is not the finale, I wonder if Kennedy will survive the culmination of the terror campaign."

Mike turned quickly, jabbing his finger in Ben's chest.

"Go home and ask your Mother the right questions. If you fail to stop this, whatever happens to Kennedy next is on you."

"You say Kennedy is safe for now? I resent your implication that my Mother is involved and expect an apology once I prove you wrong."

"You can resent the implication all you want, but tell your Mother what has happened to Kennedy and ask her if she is involved or knew of the attacks. A decent copper is supposed to have good instincts, so if someone commits a crime without concrete evidence, he needs to ask hundreds of questions if necessary to obtain that evidence. Damn it, man, ask your Mother."

Ben stalked out of the interrogation room, furious with Mike. Getting embroiled in a relationship with Kennedy was the worst thing he could have done. Sure, she had found Duke and handled him well while waiting for him to collect his dog. She had also nursed his sick dog for weeks. However, in the end, everything had fallen apart, leaving him disheartened and angry. The niggling thought that Cherise had engineered his break with Kennedy never left his mind, but he felt helpless to rectify what went wrong. Was Mike right? Was Cherise the perpetrator? Did his Mother know about the attacks and condone them? God, this relationship stuff was a nightmare.

Ben drove to his parents' house, ready to ask the questions Mike wanted the answers to. As he pulled into the driveway, Ben realised the place looked locked up. Where were his parents? A phone call was left on the message bank, and subsequent calls went unanswered. Ben texted his parents, waiting for the icon to show that his mother had read the notice, but it never came. What the dickens was going on?

Mrs Davidson called out from her front door.

"They've gone away for a week. Your mum needed a break, so they headed off early this morning."

With a nod of thanks, Ben climbed back into his car and headed for the station. There was nothing he could do about Mike's demands. Something niggled in the back of his mind. When they first had an issue with his Mother and Cherise, Kennedy asked him not to believe anything they said about her until he verified the comments. Cherise said Kennedy had let her into his house and was eager to leave, but when he thought about those statements, they didn't seem to gel with what Ben knew of Kennedy. Mike's retort to Ben's accusation that angry men were responsible confused him then and still did. He hadn't seen Kennedy with another man the day he organised to eat lunch; were Cherise's comments designed to end the relationship he and Kennedy were developing? As Ben walked through the station to his desk, the questions his memories had raised tormented him.

Coming across Mike Garrett in the break room was awkward. Neither wanted to let the other officers recognise there was an unanswered question regarding Kennedy's torment. Still, Mike wanted to hear the outcome of Ben's conversation with his parents. When the other officers left the room, Mike turned and said, "What did your Mother say?"

"I couldn't ask her as she and Dad have gone away for a week."

"Well, did you phone?"

"Yes, but the phone is out of range."

Mike completed the rest of the spiel that the telcos used. "Or turned off."

Ben looked uncomfortable. "Ah, yes."

"How often does your Mother turn off her phone?"

"Not often. Sometimes, Mum turns it to silent, but I've not known her to turn off the phone."

Mike shook his head. "Are alarm bells ringing in your head, Foster? Kennedy's house was subjected to a barrage of rocks a few nights ago, and she sustained injuries, and your Mother suddenly takes a holiday. You're wasting time in the force if you can't join the dots. I don't believe your Mother is throwing the eggs and the rocks, but she is involved, and we need to talk to her. Have your parents got a favourite spot to get away?"

"No, and like you, I feel uncomfortable about the timing of this holiday, but they're my parents, and I'm prepared to give them a break."

"Let's hope nothing happens before we speak to your mum."

Kennedy spent the remainder of the week ringing the insurance company and organising glaziers to repair the windows. She asked the workers to install hardened, tinted glass, despite the extra cost, because she could not endure another barrage of rocks. Her time at Mike's place had been like a healing balm; his Mother was kind and helpful, and each day, when she changed Kennedy's bandages, Kennedy thanked her lucky stars that Mike had taken her in. Her cuts healed, and by the end of the week, Kennedy could walk, though she needed crutches to reduce the strain on her left foot. Now she had to face the worst task: cleaning the house. Once the workers had fitted the windows, Kennedy went to her home, intending to remove the glass from her place. Cringing as she opened the front door, Kennedy did a double-take. The mess and destruction she expected to see were absent.

As she walked through the house, Kennedy could see that some items were missing, but someone had done a great job cleaning the rest of the house. Was this another of Mike's ways of helping her, or did her neighbours clean? She owed a vote of thanks to whoever was responsible for removing all the glass; it was a task she hadn't looked forward to.

Her new home had not become the haven she hoped for, and Kennedy wondered if too much had happened for her ever to feel safe here. Selling her house was not something Kennedy wanted to do, but living in fear was not an option she would choose. If she sold, would the harassment end, or would it follow her to a new destination? She could stay with Claire, but the thought of placing her sister in danger did not sit well. Kennedy sighed. She would continue to follow Mike's suggestions and hope that the perpetrator got tired of tormenting her.

Chapter 18

Kennedy watched the surrounding streets as she left the pub. Even though her tormentor seemed to have taken a break, the habit of watching her surroundings had become ingrained. Her much overdue drink with Kayla, Jill and their friends had happened tonight, and she drove away with a smile. The women might be law enforcement officers, but that didn't stop them from having a good time. They commiserated over her breakup with Ben, but they dedicated the rest of the evening to having fun.

The motion-activated lights flicked on as Kennedy drove up the driveway, and when the roller door slid open, she smiled at the relief she felt at not getting out of the car to open the door. Now that the panel beaters had returned her vehicle, she had no intention of allowing some maniac to damage it again. Alighting from the car, Kennedy collected the armful of books she had to assess that night and entered the house. Once she placed the books on her desk, she turned to return to the car when she caught movement from the corner of her eye. Swinging to face the threat, Kennedy threw her arm up to protect her face as the baseball bat swung at her. The loud crack from her arm breaking dropped her to her knees, but the madman with the baseball bat swung again. Kennedy tried to curl up to protect her body, but the bat fell with precision, shattering her hip and breaking her legs. Kennedy sobbed as the bat landed on her ribs, and that was the last thing she remembered before the pain of her injuries washed away her consciousness.

Warren heard the roller door open as Kennedy activated it. He looked out the window and caught movement in the front yard.

Warren frowned, trying to discern what had caught his attention; there was no point getting excited about a stray dog in the yard, but if someone came to harm Kennedy, he needed to investigate. Warren hesitated; he didn't want Kennedy to think he was a sticky beak, but when pounding sounds came from his neighbour's property, he grabbed the key to her house and flew out the door. Kay called out, but his fear pushed him forward.

When Warren rounded the garage, he was stunned. A blonde woman in a black cape belted Kennedy's newly repaired car with a baseball bat. When Warren yelled, the woman looked up; her face was visible before she yanked her mask on and fled. He tracked her flight and saw her climb into a small sedan before she sped away. Suddenly, it occurred to Warren that if Kennedy weren't injured, she would have chased the woman out. When he found the door open, his stomach twisted with fear. Walking quickly into the house, he spotted Kennedy instantly. She sprawled on the ground, her body and limbs bent, and the blood surrounding her made him nearly swoon. Warren cursed that he hadn't thought to bring his phone, so he hunted around on the nearby shelves before he found Kennedy's phone. The triple-zero call was frantic, and he unlocked the front door, sat next to Kennedy, and held her hand, begging her to continue breathing.

The sound of sirens split the air, and when the paramedics raced in, they asked him to move away. Police officers approached him, and he realised that they thought he had been the perpetrator.

"Can you tell us what happened here?"

"Yes, but first, can you ring Constable Garrett, even if he isn't on duty? I need someone to tell my wife I'm okay because we live next door, and she'll be worried by the sirens."

The officer agreed, and as the paramedics loaded Kennedy onto a stretcher, Warren said, "Will she be alright?"

The older of the two men shook his head. "It might be touch and go. Contacting next of kin if you know them would be a good idea."

Kay walked in as the medics wheeled the stretcher away, and she gripped Warren's arm. She wrapped her arms around him when she saw the tears in his eyes.

"I'm Constable Evans, and this is Senior Sergeant Brooks. We need to know what went on in here."

The Constable made notes as his superior asked questions.

"You mean you saw the perpetrator?"

"Yes, it was a blonde woman."

Warren couldn't give a better description because the woman wore a cloak that covered her entire body.

"I could identify her if you find her. She drove a blue Corolla hatch. I couldn't see the number plate, but it had a scratch along the back passenger door."

Just then, Mike Garrett walked in, his face ashen and his eyes moist.

"Dear God, tell me she's still alive."

The sergeant shrugged. "The paramedics think it's touch and go. They suggest we contact the next of kin. Do you know who to call?"

"Warren, don't leave until I've had a word. I will call Claire, and she can contact her parents."

Mike dialled Claire's number and, after a brief conversation, hung up.

"She's on her way now. Can we arrange for a family liaison officer to accompany Claire to the hospital? It will take ages for her parents to arrive from Wallan, and I don't want her sitting alone.'

The Sergeant nodded, and Mike turned towards Warren.

"Now, Warren, tell me what happened."

Warren repeated what he had told the other officers, and when he said he could identify the woman, Mike decided they would be better off moving to the station for formal statements. Kay said, "As much as I want to support Warren, is there any reason I can't go to the hospital?"

"Constable Evans, can you drive Mrs Gibbs to the hospital? See if they'll tell you anything about Kennedy's condition."

When they arrived at the police station, Mike called in the Commander. With Warren's description and the car details, they had cause to investigate Ben Foster's family and neighbours further.

"Call Foster in here, and let's get this bitch. When he confirms her identity, we will need a search warrant and to take the Mother into custody to find out who was helping the girl."

Ben arrived thirty minutes later, and they placed him in the same interview room Warren occupied. The Commander watched, with numerous others, from the viewing room, and Mike and Senior Sergeant Brooks sat in the interviewer's chairs. Mike raised his eyebrows, but the first comment stunned and shocked him.

"Tonight, a blond-haired woman beat Kennedy with a baseball bat. The beating was so severe that the medics said it was touch-and-go. The next of kin are gathering at the hospital."

Ben blanched and swayed in his chair.

"Dear God."

"Mr Gibbs, Kennedy's next-door neighbour, called the emergency services, but before he did, he interrupted a blond woman wearing a black cloak, and she was bashing Ms McCann's vehicle. Mr Gibbs saw her face clearly and told us that she was driving a blue Corolla hatch with a substantial scratch on the passenger-side rear door. Do you have a photo of your ex-girlfriend on your phone?"

Ben not only looked shocked but also sick. Mike thought they might need a sick bag for the man before they finished this interview. After scrolling through his phone when he passed it to Mike, he said, "My Mother loads these damn photos on my phone, thinking I'll change my mind and marry the cow."

Ben handed the phone to Mike, and when Mike passed it to Warren, he nodded.

"That's her."

After Warren's identification, things moved fast. Officers went to Ben's house to collect his Mother, and more officers went to Davidson's house to collect the Mother and arrest Cherise.

Ben sat in the break room, his head in his hands. How could his Mother be involved in terrorising Kennedy? There were no updates from the hospital where Claire, Kay and Leanne, the community liaison person, sat vigil. When his phone rang, he answered it from habit, but the frantic voice on the other end pulled him from his brooding.

"Calm down, Dad. I can't understand you if you talk so fast."

"Ben, they've arrested your Mother. Can't you do something?"

"Dad, they haven't arrested her. They've taken her into custody to ask some questions. Why don't you drive down here, and you can take her home when they finish?"

Ben wanted to speak to his Mother when she came into the station, but the Commander ordered him to go to the viewing room so that he couldn't interfere with the case. When an officer led his Mother into the interview room, Ben clenched his hands and stared at the display panel. Senior Sergeant Brooks and Mike Garrett sat on opposite sides of the table. They informed Beth Foster that they were recording the interview and asked if she wanted a solicitor present. When she declined, the officers began their questions.

"Please tell me what has happened ?"

"Mrs Foster, you are friends with Alison Davidson and her daughter, Cherise Davidson; is that correct?"

"Yes."

"For the last six months, some person or persons have run a campaign of terror against Kennedy McCann, whom I believe you have met. Tonight, someone assaulted Ms McCann so severely that the hospital holds grave fears for her life. What can you tell us about that?"

Beth Foster paled and then, in a shaky voice, said, "Can I have a glass of water? And then I will tell you what happened."

The glass of water arrived, and Beth Foster began her narration.

"Ben bought Kennedy McCann to meet our family and asked me not to invite the neighbours. I did because they are like family to me. I'm ashamed to say that Cherise, Alison and I were not welcoming, and Ben left without having lunch. A day or two later, I had lunch with Alison and Cherise, and Cherise wanted to scare Kennedy away from Ben. She started with the idea of slashing tyres and writing graffiti on her house, and even went as far as suggesting stalking her, so Kennedy was afraid. The realisation that the girl was thinking of violence against the woman scared me, and I suggested that she run a campaign of annoyance on the phone. I got Kennedy's number from Ben because I said I wanted to apologise, allowing Cherise to hang up on Ben's phone and the McCann woman's.

I knew she had escalated when she showed me the voice-changing thing, and then she laughed about egging the girl's car. I panicked and asked Alison if she knew what Cherise was doing, but she denied any knowledge. I told her to talk to Cherise and ask her to stop, but she said it was some harmless fun. I wanted to tell Ben, but I was afraid I'd be charged with something, even though I did nothing.

When Cherise visited and laughed about the damage she did to the McCann woman's home, I felt helpless. What Cherise had done was well past being annoying, and besides frightening Ben's girlfriend, Cherise was causing her financial distress. I begged her to stop, but she laughed and said she was having too much fun. Andy and I left town, and I shut off my phone because I didn't want to hear what was next on Cherise's list."

Mike Garrett shook his head in disbelief.

"You do realise if you had told Ben what was happening after the calls turned violent, Kennedy might have avoided the terror and financial hardship she endured. If Kennedy doesn't survive, you will be an accessory to murder."

Beth Foster wept, and Ben felt his heart tug at the expression of distress on her face. All the heartache Kennedy endured and the stress his Mother suffered was all because he was supposed to marry that spoiled, delusional bitch. Ben realised that while he was distracted, Garret and Brooks were wrapping up the interview.

"Mrs Foster, it goes without saying that you will remain in town so we can contact you if necessary. I'm not sure what we will charge you with if Kennedy makes a full recovery, but I do know what we will charge you with if she dies. You'd want to be praying hard for her recovery."

Ben met his Mother in the hallway and escorted her to the check-in area. He couldn't fathom what to say to his mother, so he said nothing. When his Father rushed to meet them, Beth collapsed in his arms.

Ben regarded his Father, wondering if he knew the details of what had happened, but now was not the time to ask.

"I need to go back to work, and I want to check on Kennedy's condition. We'll talk later."

Chapter 19

As Ben watched through the screen, he saw Alison Davidson seated in the chair his mother had vacated. Her usual confident demeanour was absent, and Ben wondered if she was finally aware of the chaos his mother, Cherise, and she had caused. Alison Davidson contributed little to the information the officers compiled, as Beth Foster had already covered the matter thoroughly; there was little left to discover.

Senior Sergeant Brooks sighed.

"Mrs Foster has disclosed most of what happened, but can I ask why there was a vendetta against a woman who did a good deed in returning the dog? I can't for the life of me discover the reason for the harassment of the young woman, and most everybody who has come into contact with her warms to her."

Alison Davidson glared at the officer. "You may think the bitch is all sweet and light, but she was ruining our plans. We had to dissuade her, and Cherise did that, although it got a bit out of hand towards the end."

Mike said, "What was the plan, and how did Cherise dissuade Kennedy before things got out of hand?"

Alison Davidson sighed as though the plan was so obvious she shouldn't need to spell it out.

"Beth and I are great friends. We met in primary school and have stayed close ever since. When Beth had Ben, and I had Cherise a short time later, we decided it would be great for them to marry and that we would truly become a family. Ben has been resistant, but we felt we could convince him. However, he started dating Kennedy, so she had to go. Cherise told a few lies about seeing Kennedy with another man, and she arrived at the cafe where Ben and Kennedy were to meet. When Kennedy arrived, Cherise held Ben's hand and stared lovingly into his eyes, and Kennedy ran."

Alison Davidson laughed.

"I have to give it to Cherise; she always has a way of getting what she wants."

Sergeant Brooks looked stunned, and then he recovered quickly.

"Well, I do hope your daughter wants a lengthy jail sentence, and if Ms McCann dies, she will get a life sentence. I'm sure she will be looking forward to that."

As Alison Davidson's laugh turned to a wail, Mike gestured to the constable standing guard at the door. "Get this woman out of here and put her in a holding pen. She can feel how her daughter will live for many years."

In the silence left behind by the removal of the woman, Brooks said, "Have these people not heard that arranged marriages went out years ago? Okay, let's get a coffee, check on Ms McCann and then we'll talk to the accused."

Sergeant Brooks made the coffee, and Mike contacted Leanne, the liaison officer, for an update on Kennedy's condition. Sitting here, grilling the accused made Mike fret; he wanted to be at the hospital, but he knew that if Kennedy was to receive justice, he had to do his job. According to Leanne, there wasn't much to share. The only information they had was that Kennedy was undergoing multiple surgeries, and despite Claire's desperate pleas, they could give her no more information.

When a constable led Cherise Davidson into the room, the atmosphere in the viewing room was electric.

"Ms Davidson, we are recording this interview, and I need to ask if you want a solicitor present?"

"No, I don't. Why would I? I have done nothing wrong."

Sergeant Brooks raised an eyebrow and glanced at Mike, who looked as amazed as he felt.

"Ms Davidson, I believe you met Kennedy McCann when Ben Foster invited her to a family luncheon."

"The slag who tried to steal Ben? Yes, I met her a few times."

"Shortly after that first meeting, Ms McCann started to get annoying phone calls. When the calls changed from bothersome to threatening, she contacted Constable Garrett to report the threat."

"I don't know why you are telling me this stuff. I don't care about the bitch."

Mike took over the questioning when it became apparent that Brooks felt frustrated by the woman's answers.

"Ms Davidson, we can listen to you tell falsehoods or get straight to business. Kennedy McCann started getting calls after meeting you, and when she blocked the burner phone used for those calls, the vandalism began. We have testimony from a close friend that places the blame for those attacks on you, and we have an eyewitness who saw you covered in blood vandalising Kennedy's car tonight. When you fled in your blue Corolla hatchback with the large scratch along the passenger side back door, the witness discovered Kennedy and called an ambulance."

"He must be confused."

"I didn't say the witness was a man."

"I was guessing, seeing as she has several men calling on her."

"When we searched your property, we found a black cape covered in blood, a mask and a voice synthesiser. The baseball bat you hid in your closet is covered in blood, and I'm certain lab analysis will match Kennedy's blood. What do you have to say to those charges?"

Cherise stood, and her voice echoed in the room.

"The fucking cunt deserved what she got. Ben is supposed to be my husband, and she interfered in our relationship. Yes, I did all those things, and now Ben will marry me with her out of the picture."

Sergeant Brooks stood, and the guard moved forward to help restrain the enraged woman.

"Sit down, Ms Davidson. Kennedy McCann may not be a threat to your relationship, but I doubt that Ben Foster will want to marry a woman in jail and make no mistake, your vicious crimes will result in a long period of incarceration."

Brooks gestured at the constable stationed at the door.

"Evans, will you escort this woman to the cells?"

When Cherise left the room, they could hear her voice shouting and cursing until Evans escorted her to the cells at the back of the building.

Brooks stood at the door, ready to quit the oppressive room. "God, almighty. We may have to bring in a psychologist or a psychiatrist to decide if she is competent enough to stand trial. A more delusional, violent woman I have never seen in all my years of policing."

Ben left the viewing room as the interviewing officers quit the interrogation room. Mike sympathised with the man, whose mother, her friend, and the supposed fiancé fooled him. He looked defeated, and Mike thought it might take a long time before Ben regained his confidence. If Kennedy died, he would have had her death on his conscience forever.

Mike headed for the break room, and with a cold drink in hand, he said, "Let me ring Leanne at the hospital. I'm due to knock off, so I'm heading to the hospital to keep Claire company. Do you want updates?"

Ben looked dazed but said, "Yeah, that would be good."

Chapter 20

When Mike entered the waiting room, he was stunned to see the number of people there. He had expected to see Claire and, if they had arrived, possibly her parents, but apart from the neighbours, the rest of the crowd were police officers. The female officers Kennedy had befriended were present, as were some members of the dog squad. Mike waded through the sombre group until he reached Claire. When Mike touched her on the shoulder, she turned red-rimmed eyes towards him. He only said her name, and she allowed him to embrace her as she wept quietly in his arms. With a shuddering breath, she said, "I remember the last time you did some community policing."

He gave her a wan smile before moving away from the crowd.

"Have you heard from your parents?"

Claire nodded. "They should be here soon, but I hoped to have some good news on Kennedy's condition. The last I heard, they were conducting multiple surgeries. Did you catch the person who did this?"

"Yes, but there is so much to sort out that we arrested her and threw her into jail, but apart from attempted murder, there are other charges we will bring against her."

"Does the woman even know Kennedy? Why did she harass and torture Kennedy?"

"It all had to do with Ben Foster, and I have to say I feel sorry for the bloke that this mess is all because the mothers wanted him to marry that psychopath."

Before Mike could say more, a tired-looking man in a white coat stepped into the waiting room. When he saw the crowd, he did a double-take but directed his comments to Claire.

"Miss McCann, your sister has survived the surgeries and is now in an induced coma in the ICU; if you would like to see her for a few minutes, you may."

He looked at the others and said, "Folks, I understand you are here to support Miss Claire, but this might be a long process. For now, Kennedy is in a critical but stable condition, and there is nothing anyone can do, although if you are religious, you might ask your God for some help."

As each person bade Claire goodbye, Mike, Warren, and Kay Gibbs remained. Claire looked at the lingering friends and said, "Kay, take your husband home. He has had a long, torturous day, and a few glasses of beer and a night's sleep are in order. I promise to let you know if Kennedy's condition changes."

When Kay and Warren left, the waiting room was blissfully quiet. Claire headed to the ICU, where Kennedy lay peacefully, wrapped in bandages and attached to a myriad of wires and tubes. Tears ran down Claire's face as she watched her sister, her breathing aided by a machine. The initial reports of Kennedy's injuries were troubling, but seeing them was far more traumatic. Shaken, Claire returned to the waiting room and settled next to Mike.

"Who sent Leanne to keep me company?"

"I did."

"Thank you. When I arrived, I didn't know who to speak to or what to ask, and Leanne guided me through that. I would have floundered without her, so thanks. Once everyone else arrived, I said I would be fine if she wanted to leave because I had no idea when her shift finished, but she was here all night."

The arrival of her parents interrupted their conversation, and as Claire hugged her parents, the women shed more tears. When the tears subsided, Claire introduced Mike to her parents, and they thanked Mike for keeping Claire company. He took that as his dismissal, but said. "Call me if anything changes, please."

Claire kissed him on the cheek and sent him on his way.

A week later, the doctors reduced the medication that kept Kennedy in a coma, but she hadn't woken up. Her family and friends feared that she had brain damage, but scans showed no damage. As the medical staff attempted to wake Kennedy, nothing seemed to pull her from her deep sleep. As the days wore on, Claire and her parents felt like Kennedy had made it through her surgeries but would succumb to whatever was preventing her from waking.

Claire and her parents took turns sitting with Kennedy, talking to her, reading the paper, and trying her favourite novel, but nothing worked. Her parents chatted to Claire before they left for a break, but they halted when they heard an argument in the corridor. As the arguing people reached their door, Claire looked up to see Ben with Duke on a lead, standing patiently beside his master. The large dog wore a muzzle, and once they reached the open door, Ben pulled him into the room. An angry nurse threatened to call security when Ben walked towards the bed. When Ben let Duke off the lead and removed the muzzle, Claire was sure the nurse would swoon, but he stood his ground.

"Listen, lady, with all due respect, has anything you have tried to do pulled Kennedy out of her coma? No? This visit may work, but if it doesn't, we haven't lost anything."

Ben watched as Duke circled the bed, whining. Ben felt concerned for his canine partner for the first time since he planned the visit. Kennedy's coma might stress Duke, and if she didn't wake, it might be for naught. Duke placed his front feet on the bed as the nurse continued to complain, and before Ben could stop him, Duke launched himself onto the bed. The large dog lay beside Kennedy and nudged her with his nose. Claire, her parents and Ben watched for any reaction from Kennedy. When she sighed, Ben felt like Duke might be the one to encourage her to wake. Her eyes fluttered open, and her fingers grasped Duke's long coat. Kennedy's voice, rough from lack of use, croaked as she said, "Duke."

The doctor and the security guards arrived, ready to evict Ben and Duke.

"Well, I'll be dammed. I've heard of canine therapy, but this beats all." The medico looked at the security guards and said, "We won't need you to evict this man, thank you, but I will need to check Ms McCann."

As the doctor approached the bed, Duke let out a warning growl. The doctor stepped back and glared at Ben.

"The dog needs to be muzzled."

Claire touched the doctor's arm to draw his attention to her and away from Duke.

"Doctor, Duke just did what none of us could do. Could you leave it for fifteen minutes before you check Kennedy? Ben can muzzle Duke and take him home, but I hope that the next time they visit, Ben won't have to argue his way in here."

The doctor conceded, and Ben turned to Kennedy's parents.

"We haven't met, and although Kennedy talked about Claire, I haven't met her either. I'm Ben Foster, and Kennedy spent quite some time nursing my dog back to health."

They shook hands, although Claire's welcome wasn't as enthusiastic as her parents.

"While Duke has given Kennedy the desire to wake up, this mess is your fault. She told me about what happened between you, and after all she did for you and Duke, you believed that cow you were supposed to marry. It's a pity Duke can't visit without you, but we'll have to take what we can get."

"Claire, stop."

The comment from Kennedy drew their attention back to the patient, and for the moment, they averted the trouble.

Chapter 21

It surprised Ben that Kennedy hadn't criticised him for his part in disrupting her life and the financial and physical toll it had taken on her. Her parents were more gracious than Claire, but Ben suspected they weren't privy to all that had happened between him and Kennedy. Now that she was awake, he would visit once or twice more and then leave her in peace.

Ben had taken a leave of absence, partly to help his family mend, and partly because of the embarrassment of being the centre of an investigation. Would this case haunt him for his entire professional life? Would he be overlooked for promotion when his superiors remembered this case? He scolded himself for not taking Kennedy's complaints seriously and regretted that she had to take her concerns to another officer. Despite Mike Garrett's insistence that Ben question his Mother, he deflected until it was too late. Maybe if he had related the problems Kennedy faced, his Mother might have confessed, but by the time she did, Kennedy was fighting for her life. The one positive for him, a fact that unfortunately distressed his Mother, was that the Davidson family refused to speak to their former friend.

Weeks after the police charged Cherise Davidsson with a raft of crimes, Ben received a request from his Father to attend Sunday lunch because, as a family, they needed to talk. Although his Father did not indicate what the discussion was about, Ben prayed that the Davidsons and his parents hadn't reunited. When he arrived at the house, his siblings' car was there, and upon entering, it seemed the family was not hosting the next-door neighbours. Gabe's fiancée and Ben's sister,

Sarah, helped their Mother serve the meal. He raised an eyebrow at Gabe, but he shrugged.

The meal progressed, and the conversation around the table was cordial. The gossip and information the family exchanged gave no one cause to complain. Ben knew some critical news was in the offing, but his father was never one to rush into things. Andy Foster laid down his cutlery and cleared his throat when the family finished their meal.

"The last few months have been difficult for everyone. Gabe, Sarah, their significant others and I have suffered embarrassment because of Cherise's actions. Your Mother has suffered guilt and the loss of her lifelong friend, and Ben has suffered both in his everyday life and his career. Living as we have for the last thirty years in the same house and next to people who blame us for the deranged activities of their daughter is no longer viable. Your mother and I have decided to sell the house and move into a retirement village."

Stunned silence was the response to their Father's statement, and the questions came in a flurry.

Beth Foster held her hand up to stop the questions.

"Your Father and I have discussed moving into a smaller home for many years, but the stumbling block was that I wanted Alison and Brent to join us, but they weren't keen. Now that their agreement is no longer necessary, we have decided to leave."

Ben listened to his siblings' questions as his parents answered, and his anger grew. His Mother had held back information that, if shared, could have ended the torment of Kennedy, and now they were fleeing so public opinion wouldn't touch them. What about Kennedy's injuries and the financial strain that Cherise put her in by smashing windows and vandalising her car? If reports Ben heard before he took his leave of absence were accurate, Cherise had significantly damaged the inside of Kennedy's home and her vehicle. Did his excited family realise they had jeopardised his job, and the incident would be attached to his file even if nothing was said when Ben returned to work? Every time he went for a promotion, that file would show his ineptitude in dealing with Kennedy's stalker. No longer able to listen to his parents as they restructured their lives, Ben laid down his cutlery and pushed back his chair.

"Ben dear, are you leaving?"

Ben looked at his Mother. Was she the most oblivious person in the room?

"Mother, while you and Father describe your new, exciting life, I have to return to a police station where everyone knows that if I were even half a decent copper, I would have worked out you were involved in the terrorising of Kennedy. You have almost certainly ruined my chances of advancement in the force, and what of Kennedy? I have heard not one word of compassion for the woman you allowed Cherise to victimise and terrorise. She eventually assaulted Kennedy so severely that the doctors initially feared for her survival. Her recovery could take twelve months, and how long can she support herself without her job? I understand you regret what happened, but I have never heard you apologise for your continued pressure on me to marry someone unsuited to be my wife. I might need time from my job to get my head in order, but I also need time to work on forgiving you."

As Ben left the room, he could hear his Mother's sobs, but truthfully, he couldn't find the energy to care. When they heard the slam of the front door, Andy Foster sighed.

"It never occurred to me that our excitement at starting a new chapter in our lives would upset Ben."

Sarah shook her head. "Dad, while we are pleased you have plans for the future, you should have considered what the disaster did to Ben's life and maybe not invited him to hear your plans."

Gabe nodded. "Sarah is right. In case you missed the obvious, Ben liked Kennedy greatly, and you, Mum and the Davidson women did everything possible to destroy their relationship. Have you called the hospital to check on Kennedy's progress? Have you considered sending flowers and an apology? No, you have focused on the accusations and hatred from your previous best friend and kept a low profile in town, where your friends look at you disgustedly. I am happy that you have plans, but the circumstances tend to dim the enthusiasm I can feel for you."

Sarah said, "Something Ben said raised a question. Mum, have you ever apologised to Ben for what happened?"

Beth Foster took a shuddering breath.

"I must have said sorry." She looked to her husband for validation, and he shook his head.

"No, if you have apologised, it wasn't in my hearing. It seems like we've both messed up our relationship with Ben."

Chapter 22

Kennedy's stay in the hospital was like an ongoing nightmare. As the doctors removed the tubes attached to Kennedy's body, the nurses insisted that she allow them to use a sling to help her get out of bed and to sit in a chair. Every morning, they subjected her to torture, and the pain relief, while still administered daily, only took the edge off the pain. The nurses were kind, and Kennedy understood she couldn't lie in bed for weeks. The nights were the worst, and lack of sleep caused by constant medical checks and nightmares taxed Kennedy's resolve.

It was a relief when, after a six-week hospital stay, the doctors released Kenney, and she returned to Claire's house. Unfortunately, even without the casts, Kennedy couldn't go back to work because she had rehabilitation sessions to help her regain her mobility. The McCanns had relocated for the time being to a small house near Claire's, and her parents took Kennedy to her appointments and generally fussed over her. If Kennedy thought the nurses in the hospital were strict, they were positive lambs compared to the man who ran the rehabilitation classes. Kennedy sweated and groaned daily, determined to be as fit as she was before the assault, but everyone else seemed content with the way things were. Mike was a frequent visitor, and Kennedy suspected that, although his concern for her welfare was genuine, his growing affection for Claire was also a factor.

Mike had organised a forensic cleaning company to remove evidence of her attack and clean the house thoroughly. While Kennedy would miss Warren and Kay, the thought of living in the house was something she couldn't imagine, so she called an estate agent and listed the house for sale. It was hard not to let the excitement of buying the home consume her thoughts, but her only memories of living there were tinged with regret. Some nights, Kennedy woke in a sweat, and her screaming and crying woke her sister. After weeks of nightmares, her parents insisted Kennedy make an appointment with a counsellor. Kennedy found it helpful to talk to someone who didn't have preconceived opinions relating to her torture, and when her mood plummeted, she used techniques devised by her therapist.

Kennedy hadn't seen Ben or Duke since their visits to the hospital. Ben had visited twice after his initial visit, and she missed him and Duke. Doctor Simmonds was a surprise visitor who updated her on Duke's condition and was generally good company. Even her drinking friends called to see her and wish her well, but there was no sign of Ben. She was ambivalent about seeing him. He had ignored all the warning signs about her harassment, and when he ended their relationship, he had been brutal, not allowing her time to defend herself or reject the lies Cherise spun.

Kennedy knew Ben had returned to work after his time out, and Doctor Simmonds had told her Duke was fit for service, so Ben was working with the dog squad again. When her parents left to return home, it seemed that everyone, except her, had put the trauma of the past behind them and moved on. She sometimes tried to tease out snippets about Ben, but from what little Mike told her, it appeared that he, too, had moved on. Kennedy didn't know if she would ever be the same. She had done a good turn in finding and returning Duke to Ben, only to be victimised and terrorised by a family with delusional aspirations.

The only positive of the entire debacle was that Kennedy didn't have to go through a trial because, with the testimony of the Mothers and Cherise's confession, the case was open and shut. At one point, Kennedy knew that Foster's lawyer tried to use diminished responsibility as a defence. Still, Cherise's sessions with a therapist proved that while she was delusional, she knew right from wrong, and so the reason was disallowed.

With the school year almost completed, Kennedy began to look forward to the coming year. The memories that crept out reminded her of where she was when she planned for the year she had lost. Caught up in her thoughts and snowed under with preparations for the new school year, the knock on the door startled Kennedy. A knock on the door these days caused Kennedy anxiety, so it was with trepidation that she answered the door. Ben was the one person she never expected to see again, yet here he was.

"Hello, Ben. This visit is a surprise. Do you want to come in?"

"Hello, Kennedy. This visit is a bit of a surprise to me, too.

I want to talk to you, so inside is best."

Kennedy opened the door wide, and Ben followed her through the porch to the lounge room. The scars on Kennedy's legs made him cringe, and he wondered if he could follow through with what he had to say, considering the damage their relationship had caused her.

Ben ran his hands over his face and said, "This is harder than I thought it would be."

"Would you like a drink?"

" No, no, I have to say what I came to say, and niceties will make it harder."

After taking a deep breath, Ben said, "I'm sorry, Kennedy, so damn sorry. Nothing I say will ever fix the terror and financial ruin that you've suffered because of me introducing you to my family, and my guilt compounds daily. If I had walked away before you became embroiled in my life, I could have saved you all the distress you have suffered. I knew my Mother and the Davidson women intended to try to convince me to marry Cherise, but I never believed they would go to the extent they did. My Mother and Alison Davidson are on good behaviour bonds, but even Cherise's imprisonment doesn't make what happened right."

Kennedy watched her former boyfriend as he wrung his hands in his lap and chewed his bottom lip. She knew that what happened to her would haunt her for a long time, but she didn't want it to ruin Ben's life, too.

"Ben, let's put the hurt aside for a minute; I want to know what happened between us that caused you to move Duke to the kennels and cut me out of your life. The last time we had contact, you asked to meet for lunch, but when Mike and I arrived, you were holding Cherise's hand and looking deeply into her eyes. You were mad if you thought I was sticking around after that."

"So you were with Mike?"

"Yes. I wanted to talk about what happened the night before, and Mike wanted to encourage you to discuss the vandalism with your Mother. We thought two birds with one stone. Why?"

"Because Cherise told me she saw you with a police officer, hugging and kissing."

"So, even after I asked you to talk to me if those women made comments about me, you believed her? I'll tell you what I know, and then you can have your say. That mad cow who was supposed to be your wife used your Mother's key and let herself in. As soon as I heard the key in the lock, I knew it wasn't you because Duke went ballistic. She told me she was making you a home-cooked meal, and we got into an argument. That's when she called me a c*nt, and I realised that she was the voice on the other end of the phone. I settled Duke and left, hoping you'd ring, but you texted instead. Mike came with me that day because I was at the station making a statement about the graffiti on the road outside my place, and once I realised who the perpetrator was, we decided to talk to you together."

Ben rested his head in his hands. After a moment's silence, he said, "Cherise told me that you opened the door for her and when she said she was making a meal, you were relieved because you needed time away from Duke and me. It hurt that you would say that, so I texted you. The next day, Cherise sat at the table before you arrived and told me I was wasting my time waiting for you because she saw you alight from a police cruiser, and the officer hugged and kissed you. She took my hand, and the look I gave her was trying to decide if she was lying. When you didn't arrive, I knew what she said was true. And I called you to stop our arrangement."

"And your phone call was so brutal and abrupt that you gave me no opportunity to defend myself."

"Can you ever forgive me?"

Kennedy blew out a breath.

"I don't blame you for what those women did to me. You were a victim, too. I understand that we all want to think well of our parents, but if you had connected the dots and taken Mike's advice to discuss my harassment with your Mother, she might have come clean then."

"Will you come and visit Duke and me? He misses you, and so do I."

Kennedy stood momentarily and said, "What about your mum and the Davidson woman? What will your family say? I can't repeat what I've endured again."

"My parents have moved to a retirement village and have no contact with the Davidsons, who blame my Mother and me for what happened. My Mother knows that I will not tolerate interference in my life, and my Dad told me that I was a fool to let you go. The night the guy stabbed Duke, Dad told me he despaired of me when you had done so much for me, and he guessed that Cherise had been instrumental in splitting us up. Gabe and Sarah dressed my Mother down about her selfishness and her part in your treatment. I'd say my family are all on board."

"Maybe we could postpone meeting family for now and see whether we can make this, whatever this is, work."

Epilogue

When Ben and Kennedy reconnected, they moved slowly as they became reacquainted. Kennedy was initially hesitant, unwilling to put her heart out to be broken again. They socialised with other police officers and their neighbours, but the question of meeting Ben's parents arose six months after they reunited. Ben had met Kennedy's parents when she was hospitalised and then again when Claire married Mike. It seemed time had run out to accept the long-standing invitation extended by Ben's parents.

Using Ben's weekend off, Kennedy and Ben travelled to Ellerton to visit his parents and siblings. The retirement village the Fosters now resided in had a sizeable dining room that residents could reserve for private use, and it was there that they held their dinner. Kennedy wasn't too nervous about meeting Mr Foster or Ben's siblings, but the thought of coming face-to-face with the woman who was instrumental in her terrifying ordeal two years ago made her quake. Ben knew how nervous Kennedy was and prayed that his mother would be gracious if she couldn't manage to be friendly.

When they pulled into the parking lot, Kennedy was surprised by the extensive gardens. Her preconceived idea of what this place would look like was nothing like she imagined. The buildings were neat and modern. The area surrounding the homes contained tennis courts, a bowling green and a swimming pool. The Fosters may not be wealthy, but they have undoubtedly fallen on their feet in their new home. Ben held Kennedy's hand as they walked towards the dining room and stood near her as they introduced themselves. Kennedy liked Mr Foster and Gabe, Sarah, and her husband, Mark, who were welcoming and friendly. Steeling herself for the introduction to Beth Foster, Kennedy plastered a smile and looked at the woman who had caused her so much angst. The introduction was awkward, and Kennedy was unsure if she should speak first or if that was up to Beth Foster. Kennedy noticed the woman's eyes drifted to where she and Ben had their hands entwined, and the woman gave a slight grimace. The other diners were tense, and Kennedy could feel Ben's tension, so she decided that if she were to continue her relationship with Ben, she had to accept them.

"Mrs Foster, it is nice to meet you again. I hope we can let bygones be bygones and move forward."

Beth Foster smiled. "Thank you, dear. I was afraid my behaviour might make you hostile towards me, and that would make Ben unhappy. I remember you telling me once before that I should want my children to be happy, and it seems my son is happiest when he is with you."

Everybody seemed to breathe again as though they were waiting for the conversation between Beth Foster and Kennedy to conclude. Kennedy enjoyed the dinner she shared with Ben's family and invited them to join Ben and her parents for a meal before school resumed.

TWO YEARS LATER

KENNEDY HOPED FOR MORE at the beginning of their relationship, but getting caught up in Ben's weird family dynamic proved more problematic than she could ever have imagined. After being beaten within an inch of her life, Kennedy kept her wits about her the second time around. As she had lain in her hospital bed two years ago and struggled through rehabilitation classes, she never expected to end up here. Knowing that she would be a married woman within the hour made her equal parts excited and terrified. Did all women feel like this before their weddings, or was her terror a premonition of things to come?

"Am I doing the right thing?"

Claire smiled at her sister.

"I felt the same. I couldn't decide if I wanted to throw up or if I wanted to run screaming from the gazebo. All those feelings disappeared when I walked towards Mike, dressed in his parade uniform. He was so handsome, and his smile reassured me. You may have had a more challenging path than most couples, but you have persevered, and the fact that you are here today speaks volumes about your enduring connection. Put away the nerves and go meet your man."

Claire spoke from experience. Her relationship with Mike developed quickly after Kennedy's traumatic summer, but it wasn't always smooth sailing. When Kennedy realised Claire's feelings for Mike, she laughed at the insanity of both her sister and her becoming involved with police officers. Claire's wedding, nearly a year ago, was a small affair compared to Kennedy's traditional white wedding.

Claire helped Kennedy with her veil, which was quite a task with her extended belly, and then she left her sister as her Father entered the room.

"Are you ready? Your man is so nervous; he thinks you might have second thoughts and run from the church screaming."

Kennedy smiled. "I'm ready. Let's do this thing."

.

Also by Robyn C Rye

Farnsworth Sisters
Marrying a Rogue
Rescuing Hannah

The Buckingham Sisters
Lady Maggie's Challenge
Layla's Unwanted Husband

The Evans Family
Sometimes Love is not Enough
Still the One
Moving Forward

Standalone
One More Chance
Lady Jayne's Reputation
Third Time's the Charm
Can't Stop Loving You

The Marriage Scam
An Unlikely Match
Searching For You
The Unexpected Suitor
The Lady and the Duke
Starting Over
An Unforgettable Stranger
The Duke's Revenge
The Temporary Wife
Against The Odds
Betrayed
No Good Turn Goes Unpunished
Lady Eloise's Soldier
Lillian's Forbidden Beau
Remember Me
Always Second Best
When One Door Closes
Coming Home to You
Chasing Shadows
Fool Me Once
Deserting Lady Audrey
My Unlikely Saviour
Lies and Deception
A New Beginning
Julia's Second Chance
The Hidden Enemy
The Maiden's Redemption
Miss Elizabeth's Season

www.ingramcontent.com/pod-product-compliance
Lightning Source LLC
Chambersburg PA
CBHW020610160726

47991CB00002BA/714